MW00657042

Unexpected Odds

New York Times Bestselling Author

KAYLEE RYAN

UNEXPECTED ODDS
Copyright © 2020 Kaylee Ryan
All Rights Reserved.
This book may not be reproduced in any manner whatsoever without the written permission
of Kaylee Ryan, except for the use of brief quotations in articles and or reviews.

This book is a work of fiction. Names, characters, events, locations, businesses and plot are
products of the author's imagination and meant to be used in a fictitious manner. Any
resemblance to actual persons, living or dead, or actual events throughout the story are purely
coincidental. The author acknowledges trademark owners and trademarked status of various
products referenced in this work of fiction, which have been used without permission. The
publication and use of these trademarks are not authorized, sponsored or associated by or with
the trademark owners.

The following story contains sexual situations and strong language. It is intended for adult
readers.

Cover Design: Sommer Stein, Perfect Pear Creative Covers
Cover Photography: Wander Aguiar
Model: Jonny James
Editing: Hot Tree Editing
Proofreading: Deaton Author Services
Formatting: Integrity Formatting

Prologue

KENT

Tilting my beer to my lips, I peer over the bottle at the clock on the wall. Ten minutes after eleven. I'm late. Hell, I'm beyond late. I was supposed to meet her at seven. She goes back to school tomorrow, and this is our last night together. I told her I would be there, but instead, I'm here, sitting at Bottom's Up, having a few beers with the guys. All of them none the wiser that I'm supposed to be meeting my... regular hookup? She's not my girlfriend; we don't label what we are.

Not really.

This thing between us has been going on for over two years now. She was home from college break, her and a group of friends were here at Bottom's Up having a few beers, we hit it off, I took her home. She stayed. We ended up spending the weekend in bed, and she went back to school. She came home for spring break and I ran into her at the gas station of all places. We hooked up while she was here, then she went back to school.

You get the idea. That's how things have been between us for the last two years. That is until this summer. The last few weeks specifically. It's starting to feel like... more. Fuck me, but I know it's more, and instead of facing these feelings head-on, I'm drinking with the guys, and I know

1

without a doubt she's there waiting for me. I was supposed to meet her at a bed and breakfast a few towns over. I was dressed, ready to go and dreading this being the last time I see her until Christmas break. My heart was racing and my palms were sweating because I know, I know what she means to me. I'm just too afraid to admit it. Ridge called as soon as I was walking out the door, said the guys were getting together tonight for a few beers. They don't know about her, and it gave me an excuse to delay saying goodbye to her.

I don't want to say goodbye.

My gut twists when I think about not seeing her for months. I don't know why this time is different, but it's more, and I don't do more. At least I haven't. Me being here proved her mother right. I'm no good for her. She deserves better—that's what she tells her. We've been sneaking around so she doesn't have to hear that shit. Then again, I haven't told anyone about her, so again, maybe her mom is right. She's not a dirty little secret and shouldn't be treated as such.

"What's up with you?" Mark asks.

"Nothing. Just tired." I hide the truth.

"You've been helping your dad a lot lately," Tyler comments.

"Yeah, he's been cleaning out the old barn." It's not a lie. Dad has been cleaning out the old barn this summer, and I've helped him a time or two when he needed it, but those other times, I was with her.

"What's he going to do with that old thing?" Tyler asks.

"Mom's trying to talk him into turning it into a venue, you know, for weddings and stuff like that."

Ridge chuckles. "You think she'll get her way?"

"Nah, my guess is that Dad's going to turn it into an art studio for her. She loves to paint, and if you were to add some windows to the back, the view is the perfect backdrop. I've heard Mom tell us that a thousand times."

My parents had a horse; Harry was his name. He was a Tennessee Walking Horse and Mom's baby. He passed about a year ago, and they've decided no more horses, or animals at all in fact. They want to travel. So Dad's been selling off the tack and tearing out the stalls. He doesn't have to tell me that he's making it a special place for her, that's just Dad. That's who he is. Mom is the love of his life, and there is no limit to what he'll do to see her smile.

"She's going to love that." This from Tyler.

"Yeah." I finish off my beer, pull a twenty out of my wallet, and place it on the table. "I'm going to head home. I told him I would be by early in the morning to help." That's not a lie. I've made her wait long enough, and I'm an asshole for it. I should have owned up and gone straight to her. Told her how I feel about her, and that this feels like more. Maybe we can try being official?

"You need us?" Mark offers.

"Sure, you know the way. I'm going to get there around nine." Her flight leaves at eight. I mentally calculate how much time I wasted tonight and hate myself for it. "Stop by whenever." With that, I'm out the door. Before I've even made it to my truck, I try calling her, but it goes to voice mail.

"Hey, it's me. I know I'm late. I'm on my way." I toss my phone in the cup holder and point the truck to the outskirts of town. She said she wanted to talk to me, her tone said it was serious, but I already know what she was going to say. She's in deep. We both are. Only difference is I'm too big of a coward to admit it. At least I was about four hours ago. Maybe it's the alcohol, but then again, maybe it's just her and the thought of her not being mine. I'm going to grovel and tell her how I feel. It's time to face this like a man, treat her like she deserves to be treated. I was raised better, and my momma would kick my ass if she knew what I did tonight.

I make it to the B&B but don't see her car. I call her again. No answer. Trudging inside, I ask if she checked in. I listen as the clerk tells me that she was here, but she left a few hours later. I give a curt nod and head back to my truck.

I try calling her again, and again, and again. I'd go to her place, but her parents don't approve of me. I'm too "small town" for their liking. Hell, they live in the same damn small town, but I'm not good enough for their daughter. Part of me thinks that's why I haven't told her what she means to me, but that's just a small part. If I'm being honest, there is always this worry in the back of my mind that she's going to wake up and realize she's had her fun with me, and this is all going to end. I can't see her parents ever approving of me with my blue-collar job and my inked-up skin. Back then, I only had a few tattoos. If her mom could see me now, I can only imagine what she would think. I see the disapproval in their eyes the handful of times I've met them. She's never given me any reason to think otherwise, but there's the lingering doubt that has kept my walls in place.

Until this summer.

I call her again. This time, I leave another message. "Hey, it's me. I'm sorry I was late. I'm here, but the B&B said you checked out. I'll be up for a few hours. You can come over, or I'll meet you. Just… call me." Another round of guilt hits me. If I was honest to my friends about her, if they knew what she meant to me, I wouldn't be here right now. I would be with her in my arms where she belongs. Instead, I kept her from them, and I know damn well they would be up my ass about standing her up. I've learned my lesson. I just need to find her. To tell her I'm sorry and I'll shout it to the world.

I drive past her parents' place, and sure enough, her little white Volkswagen sits out front. It takes herculean effort to not pull into her drive, but I hold strong and drive on past, headed home.

I call her again when I get into the house, but I know it's no use. She's pissed. As she should be. I'll call her in the morning. I'm a dick. I hate that I won't get to see her before she leaves, but I only have myself to blame. Somehow, I'm going to make this right. I can't wait until winter break. It's not something I want to do over the phone, but that's the only option since my dumb ass might have fucked up the best thing to ever happen to me.

It's time to man up and tell her how I feel.

It's time I admit to her, and to myself, that I'm in love with her.

Chapter 1

Delaney

I've checked my list a million times to make sure I have everything. This is the first time I've traveled alone, and I'm both excited and nervous. I'm an adult, so you'd think something as simple as a plane ride from California to Tennessee wouldn't be an issue. Well, you'd be wrong, at least when it comes to me.

"You all packed?" my mother asks from my doorway.

Yes, I still live with my parents, well, my mom. We lost my dad three years ago to a heart attack. It was hard for both of us, in different ways, and even though I could move out, I'm still here. I hate the thought of leaving her alone. Besides, she's done so much for me. Been there for me when there was no one else.

"Yes." I hold up my list that's been checked off multiple times.

Mom chuckles. "You never used to be a list maker. I'm glad you've found a process that helps you."

I hold up my notepad and close the cover, sliding it into my purse. "Never leave home without it."

"You know, the iPad I bought you would be so much more efficient than all those paper lists." She furrows her brow. She can't grasp that I prefer putting pen to paper. "I mean, aren't I the one who's supposed to be afraid of technology?"

"I'm not afraid of technology, Mother." I hold up my e-reader as proof. "I just prefer the paper method. There is just something about being able to mark items off a list and then tossing it in the trash once it's complete."

"To each their own, I guess." She sighs heavily. "I still don't understand why you insist on going. I hate that town, and that house for that matter."

"Because Grandma and Grandpa left it to Dad, who left it to me, and it's only right I'm there to oversee the renovations. And you never have told me why you hate the house, and the town so much."

"Small town living isn't for me. The house, it's too... I don't know... I just was never fond of it. And I still can't believe your father left it to you. I tried to get him to sell years ago."

"Because Grandma and Grandpa owned it? Is that why you never liked it?" I ask, even though I know I'm right. She never really got along well with my father's parents. They passed away when I was in high school, and as soon as I graduated, Dad was able to somehow convince Mom to move. It didn't last long.

"They always looked at me as being beneath them." I raise my eyebrows in surprise at her words. "You'll never know how that feels until you experience it for yourself. To know the family of the man you love thinks you're not good enough. It's tragic," she says dramatically—in a way that only my mother can.

"You hardly seem traumatized."

"You don't know," she says, giving me a pointed look.

I hate it when she does that. Always dropping reminders. "Well, I didn't expect for the renovators to start this week, but it's worked out. You're coming this weekend, right? I scheduled your flight."

"And where are we staying?" She sighs. She's acting as if the world is coming to an end.

"At the house of course."

"What? Why would we do that? There used to be a decent hotel. Surely we can stay there."

"Mother, why would we? Grandma and Grandpa's house is huge. There's plenty of room for us to stay there."

"During renovations?" she asks, appalled.

"Correct me if I'm wrong, but didn't we do the same thing here after Dad died? You went through some kind of 'must change my surroundings' thing. We survived and this house isn't half the size as theirs."

She rolls her eyes. We both know I'm right. We lost Grandma and Grandpa within a few months of each other. I swear Gramps's heart was broken without Grams and that's why we lost him. I'm a romantic at heart, and I probably read way too many romance novels, but that's what I like to believe.

"Fine."

"Perfect. Now I need to do one last check that I have everything, then head out so I don't miss my flight."

"Delaney," my mom whispers. I look up to find her wringing her hands together and what looks like dread on her face. "Those people in that town, they never liked me. Just… stay away from them, all right? Do what you need to do with the attorney and the construction crew and just… lay low. I don't want you having to deal with what I did."

"Mom, you're paranoid. Everything is going to be fine. Besides, that was years ago and since when has it been the 'people' in town? You just said it was Grandma and Grandpa?"

"It's everything. Just promise me. Hang out at the house, and don't—" She stops as if she's trying to find the right words. "Just… don't venture out alone. At least wait until I arrive on Thursday."

"You know you could come with me now."

"Oh, and miss bridge with the ladies next week? I couldn't. Besides, Martha is having a knee replacement, and we're not going to be playing for the next several weeks. This is my last chance to see them all together until we pick back up."

I fight the urge—and it's a strong one—to roll my eyes. Heaven forbid something more important than hanging out with the ladies to play bridge comes up in her life. However, it works out for other reasons as well, so I can't be too upset with her. "Fine. I'll see you on Thursday." I lean in and give her a hug. Grabbing my suitcase, I exit the room. I need to see the girls and then bust ass to the airport.

By the time the plane lands, I've managed to calm my nerves. I don't know why traveling by myself has me so worked up. It's not like I've never flown before. I think it's Mom and all her "the people of that town are mean, blah blah blah." I'm paraphrasing but it's the same concept. She has me freaked out for nothing. Everyone has been friendly on this little adventure. Case in point: I'm waiting on my rental car, and I've been asked no less than three times if I'd like something to drink. Mom had me thinking the worst… like everyone in the state of Tennessee are assholes. That's simply not the case. And some of them, they have these Southern accents that I could listen to all day. As I sit and wait for my rental, I pull the letter out of my purse that Dad's attorney gave to me, along with the deed to my grandparents' estate.

> *Delaney,*
>
> *Their hope was to always keep this property in the family. The decision is yours. I won't make it for you. My one request is that you go spend some time there. Enjoy the town and the people before you decide.*
>
> *Forever in my heart.*
>
> *Dad*

Folding the letter, I slide it back into my purse. I don't know why he felt so strongly about me visiting, but it's a small concession as a last request. I swallow hard, fighting back my tears. I miss him so much.

"Ma'am." A young guy who doesn't look a day over eighteen approaches me. "We have your SUV ready for you. Can I take your bags?"

"That's not necessary." I give him a kind smile. "Thank you." Standing from my chair, I follow along.

He nods. "It's the black Dodge Durango." He points to where the SUV sits.

"Thank you." Wheeled baggage in hand, I make my way to the car. After tossing my bag into the back seat, I take my time adjusting the driver's seat and the mirrors. Ever since my accident, I've been extra cautious when driving. If my mother had her say, I'd never drive again.

You can't live your life in fear. At least that's what I keep telling myself. Punching the address into the SUV's GPS, my hands at ten and two, I head toward my destination.

First impression? Tennessee is beautiful. With all the mountains and the trees, how could anyone hate it here? A quick glance at the dash tells me I'm close. Just one more mile. My hands flex on the steering wheel from my tight grip, my nerves getting the best of me—well, my mother's nerves.

"You've arrived at your destination," the female voice of the GPS informs me.

Turning on my signal, I pull into the long driveway. There's a metal arch held by two brick pillars declaring Nottingham Estate. An odd sensation washes over me, one I can't name. It's as if this place is home to me, but that's not the case. My home is in California. It has to be nostalgia as this was Gram and Gramps's home. Then again, maybe it's because my father left it to me in the will. Something my mother was unaware of and is still angry about to this day.

I'm not sure what Dad's motivation was, and why he left it to me, but his specific instructions were clear. The property was mine. It was mine to do with as I wished, after I personally oversaw the remodel. His hope, per the letter he left with his will, was that this will be my home, but if I decide after spending time here that it isn't the case, he would be okay with me selling, but only if that's what I want to do.

Mother was livid, of course. She insisted we put it on the market as is, and I quote, "We never have to step foot in that godforsaken town." After just the drive across town, and now that I'm here sitting in the circle drive staring at my family's history, I know without a shadow of a doubt that there are reasons, other than the excuses that she's given me, that she hates this town, this house.

Grabbing the keys to the rental, my phone, and purse, I climb out of the SUV, shutting the door. I stretch my sore muscles and take a deep breath of the clean mountain air. The cool air burns my lungs, but in a good way. No smog. Nothing like California, and I love it already. My eyes rake over the home that's been neglected for the past few years, and even though the landscaping is overrun, and the paint is chipping, even I can see the beauty in the home before me. Excited to see the inside, to see what I'm dealing with, I take a step forward when I hear a car approach. Turning, I shield my eyes from the sun and watch a black sedan park behind my rental.

9

An older gentleman climbs out of the car. He pulls at his pants that are already being held up by suspenders, that peek out under his coat, as he approaches me. "Ms. Nottingham?" he asks. His hand is already thrust forward in greeting, waiting for me to shake it.

"Delaney." I take his offered hand.

"Harold Garcia, it's nice to officially meet you."

"You as well. Thank you for meeting me here."

"Of course. Have you been here long?"

"No, I actually just pulled in."

"Beautiful place." He nods toward the house.

"It really is." There is snow on the treetops and on the mountains that are in the distance, yet they seem so close at the same time. It's almost like a painting or a Christmas card. Even rundown the place is gorgeous.

"Well, shall we get started? I have the construction crew scheduled to start tomorrow. Your mother emphasized that time was of the essence. She indicated that you want the renovations done as quickly as possible to get the property on the market."

"That's my mother, not me. I own the property and… I'm not so sure I'm selling it." My mother is insistent that's the outcome, but I've never been confident on the idea. Now, just being here, that feeling is stronger than ever. I can't explain it.

"Oh, well, all right. Shall we take a look? We can do a walkthrough and discuss what you want changed. Your mother—" he starts, but the look I flash him shuts him up.

"Doesn't have a say." I feel defiant in my words, but the pull that this place has on me is not only instant but strong. "I am the owner, and it's my money that's paying you and the contractor," I remind him. Sure, it's my inheritance from my father, but it's mine, not my mother's. Just something else that she was not happy about when my father passed away.

"Yes. Yes." He nods vigorously. "Shall we get started?" he asks.

I smile at him. "Yes." Digging the key to the house from my purse, I take the steps up the front porch one at a time, careful that they might be slick. Once I've slid the key into the lock, I slowly push open the door and step inside. My eyes scan the foyer as I take one step then another until I'm standing inside the living room. If it were not for the thin layer of dust and the musty smell, I wouldn't be able to tell that a family didn't live here.

There are still family photos on the mantel, a throw lying over the back of the couch, and a pair of slippers sitting next to the coffee table. It's as if my parents just took what they had to, and left the rest. Why would they do that?

"Oh," Mr. Garcia says, coming to stand next to me. "I wasn't expecting this. I just assumed it would be empty."

"Yeah, so did I." I turn to look at him. "What does this mean for the renovation? Will it set us back?"

"Let me make a few calls. However, I think first and foremost, we need to do a walkthrough and decide what needs to be replaced or repaired. That will tell us what we're dealing with when it comes to the personal belongings and how to handle moving them."

"Good idea." I look down at the sage green carpet that appears to be something from the seventies. "Um, the carpet has to go." I laugh.

Mr. Garcia scribbles on his notepad. "Carpet, got it."

"I think the entire house could do with a new coat of paint on the inside and out." It's hard to tell with all the dust and cobwebs.

"Right. I'm not sure if the construction crew will handle the outside painting but if not, I'll find someone who will." He's quick to agree as his pen rushes across the page taking notes.

We spend the next hour going from room to room, deciding what needs to be updated. With each room, I fall even more in love with the house.

"Right, so we're updating all the flooring, all the bathrooms, the kitchen is a complete makeover, and paint on all the walls." Mr. Garcia reads off his list.

"Yes. For now." I smile big, and he returns it with one of his own.

"Oh, and new paint and landscaping for the outside. Although, since it's January, that might have to wait until spring."

"That's fine," I assure him. "Like I said. I'm not sure I even want to sell. Maybe we'll keep it for a vacation home." His eyes widen, and I can't help but laugh. This house is gorgeous and huge, too huge to be a simple vacation home. "Maybe a bed and breakfast," I say, thinking out loud.

"I'm sure you will figure it out. And when your mother calls?" he asks hesitantly.

"I'll handle my mother. This is my home, not hers. It's my money we're spending. Not hers." I remind him yet again. Once Tillie Nottingham gets her claws in you, it's hard to get them to retract. I need Mr. Garcia and anyone he hires to understand that I'm the homeowner and the person in charge of the decisions. I've sat on the sidelines to my mother for years. I needed her, but I'm a grown woman, and while I appreciate all that she's done for me, it's time for me to start making my own choices. Consequences be damned.

Chapter 2

KENT

I'm sitting in the middle of the living room floor surrounded by my nieces and nephews. Ryder, the youngest at three months, is in my arms, his little eyes darting all around as he takes in the loudness that is his big sister and his cousins.

"Uncle Kent, I'm big like you," Knox says, scooting over to sit next to me, his legs crossed at the ankles like mine.

"My man," I say, holding my fist out for him. He bumps it like we taught him to when he was just a tiny thing. He's the oldest of this brood, and I feel sorry for Everly, Daisy, and Finley. He's definitely going to be the protector for his baby sister and cousins. My guess is that Beckett, Benjamin, and even Ryder are going to follow right along in his footsteps. My brothers are raising their sons right.

The girls are putting bows in my hair from their gifts while the boys and I play trucks. Ryder is my sidekick, so he's currently chewing on my truck. It's soft, unlike the others, but hey, I'm the cool uncle, so he had to be involved.

There's a smile on my face as I interact with the kids, but all the while my mind is racing. Ridge said we're starting a job at the Nottingham Estate. It's been almost five years since I've been there. Not long after my visit there, the Nottingham family moved away to California to be closer to their daughter.

"Uncle Kent." Finley pats me on the cheek. "I'm a pwincess." She twirls in her little pink dress that Santa brought her.

"You ladies, all three of you, are beautiful princesses," I tell them. I can't play favorites, and all the girls are dressed up like princesses. I can tell the wives coordinated. More than likely they went shopping together.

I love how our group is growing. Every one of my brothers has found their perfect match, and their littles… they have their tiny hands rooted deep in my chest and around my heart. The guys tell me it's different when it's your own, but I don't know how that could be. I love these kiddos as if they were mine.

And today, I'm thankful to have them. Memories invade my thoughts, but they don't seem to notice, not like their parents would. Instead of trying to make small talk while my mind is pulling up every memory—no, that's not right; it's more like every second, every minute, every hour, every breath I ever took with her—that's what my mind is flashing like a movie reel. Not that this is a new occurrence. I've been thinking about her a lot lately. Hell, I never stopped thinking about her.

Delaney Nottingham was the one who got away. I was the dumb fuck who let her slip through my fingers. I had her, and then one day, she was just… gone. She never came home again, and her parents moved away.

I stood her up that final day. I didn't treat her the way she'd deserved to be treated. I fucked up and lost her. It was then I admitted to myself what I had known all along. I loved her. Up until that final night, I'd tried to show her. I worshiped her body, showing her with my actions what she meant to me. They say actions speak louder than words, and I think they do. Which is why my actions that final night, pushed her away. One night of not showing up, of not giving her the love and respect she deserved and here I am, almost five years later, without her.

Lesson learned.

Mara sits next to me on the floor and Finley climbs into her lap. "You need one of those," she says, leaning her shoulder against mine.

"Yeah, maybe one day." The problem is the only woman I've ever imagined having this kind of life with is Delaney. I'm sure she's married with kids by now. Kids that aren't mine.

"Well, until you meet the woman who's going to knock you off your feet, you're a good uncle. Think of it as training for when that day comes." Mara smiles as she reaches over and runs her index finger over Ryder's tiny hands.

I nod like I'm supposed to, hiding the pain that slices through me. It's been almost five years, and no one has even come close to Delaney in my eyes. I've accepted my fate as always being the cool uncle and never the daddy. I glance down at Ryder, who's staring up at me. My heart squeezes in my chest as I think about what I lost. What I fucked up. Maybe one day my heart will heal, but I'm not holding my breath.

"That's my baby brover," Finley says, pointing at Ryder.

"I know. You know what else I know?" I lower my voice. She shakes her head and I crook my finger, telling her silently to come closer. She glances at Mara and then leans into me. "I know that you're the best big sister in the world."

Her eyes light up and she grins. "That's whats my daddy tells me too." Her eyes are wide as she jumps off her mom's lap and rushes to Seth. He sees her coming and bends down to catch her. He hugs her, places a kiss on her cheek, and then goes back to whatever conversation he and Mark are in.

I envy my brothers. I'm not going to say I'm jealous, because I couldn't be happier for all four of them. They have wives who are their perfect counterpart and their kids… they're little versions of them.

The rest of the kids wander away, and I'm left sitting on the floor with Mara. "What's going on?"

I turn to look at her. "Nothing. Why?" Lies.

"You just seem like there's something bothering you."

That's something else. The guys and I have been best friends since we were kids—brothers by bond and lifelong friendship. Their wives, aside from Reagan, are new additions to our brood, but they are all intuitive as fuck. There is no hiding anything from any of them. "Nope."

"Right." She chuckles. "When you're ready to talk about it, you have a room full of people who are willing to listen."

I know she's right. The sad part about that is that I had that same core group, minus the wives all those years ago. I should have fessed up to what I had with Delaney. I should have never blown her off to have drinks with the guys. They would have understood. I was young, dumb, and too big of an idiot to realize what I was throwing away. I can tell you this. If by some chance one day I'm lucky enough to find that again… If I'm lucky enough to find that one person who captures my body, my heart, and my mind, I'm going to show her, tell her, and love the fuck out of her for as long as I live. I won't make the same mistake twice.

❋❋❋

I've been dreading this day since Ridge announced that we would be working on the Nottingham Estate. Luckily with the holidays, I had a few days to get my head in order. Well, that was the plan, but pulling up to the house, my body stiffens. I'm immediately taken back to the day I drove up the winding driveway, climbed out of my truck, and knocked on the door. Tillie Nottingham answered and turned her nose up at me.

"Yes, can I help you?"

"Yes, ma'am. I was wondering if you could give me Delaney's address."

"Why on heaven's earth would I do that?" She scoffs and glances down at my dirty boots. I've just left the jobsite after a long day and came straight here.

"She's not answering her phone. I need to speak to her." It's been weeks since I've talked to her.

"Oh, dear, you didn't think she was serious about you, did you?" She pauses, and the expression on my face must say it all. "Oh." She slaps her hand over her mouth. "You did. That's so… sweet. I'm sorry to be the one to tell you, Delaney got back together with an old flame. They're moving in together, so you see, you showing up on her doorstep isn't a good idea."*

"If you could just tell me where I can find her." I'm kicking myself in the ass for never going to visit her at school.

"Delaney has moved on, and there's hope of a grandchild in my future. She doesn't want to see you, Kenton. Please leave." It's with those parting words she shuts the door in my face.

"Kent." Mark waves his hand in front of my face. "You planning on working today, or you just want to sit in the truck and freeze your ass off?"

"Fuck off," I murmur, and he laughs as we climb out of the truck. Looking up at that front door, the same door that was slammed in my face, I know I gave up too easily. I should have turned over every stone, knocked on every damn door at that college until I found her. What's that saying, I wish I would have known then what I know now? Yeah, that one hits the nail on the head.

Ridge is already standing at the door, and when he presses the doorbell, I hold my breath. It's not her. I know it's not her. Ridge said that the family attorney contacted him in regard to the renovation. The estate has been vacant for almost five years.

The family simply up and left.

Bracing myself on the pillar of the front porch, I stand behind Ridge, Tyler, Mark, and Seth as we wait for someone to answer the door. It's as if it happens in slow motion. The handle turns and the door pulls open. I want to close my eyes. I want to look away, but I can't. I watch, breathless, as an older gentleman appears. My breath whooshes from my lungs, and my shoulders sag. Although it's not with relief, it's disappointment.

I wanted it to be her.

I can hear Ridge talking to him, and he invites us in. He's been put in charge of the renovations, as we already know—appointed by the family. Following them inside, I take a look around. I've never been here. It was too risky with her parents and the staff. They hated me, so Delaney always ended up at my place, or at the lake, sleeping under the stars. And on the nights when it was too cold at the lake, we would go to the B&B. Just another place for us to be together. Delaney always thought it was romantic.

Never here.

My eyes take in my surroundings. The home is huge, but it's not over the top with decorations. I always envisioned it as a castle, but it's not. Maybe in size, but that's it. The living room is a light beige with dark brown furnishings. It appears to be a solid oak trim. There are family photos plastered all around, as if the family still lived here. If not for the dusty furniture, I would think they did. I'm not really sure, structurally, what is needed, and I'm sure if I had been paying attention, I would know. I can't seem to stop taking it all in. I can see her here, feet propped up on the couch, her blonde hair splayed out on the cushions. She only lived here for a couple of years. It was her grandparents' home, and when they passed, her parents inherited it. I guess that's why it was so easy for them to up and walk away.

I can't believe I'm here. In her childhood home. What are the odds that out of all the contractors, they picked Beckett Construction? This job is unexpected, and the past is coming full circle into my present. At least the memories are—the ones I try to keep locked away. I remember her—her laugh, her smile, those never fade. But the times we shared, I try to lock that shit up tight. They surface a few times a year, but for the most part, I can move forward each day without the loss of her in my life threatening to take me under.

Most days.

"So, as you see, the home needs some updating in order to be placed on the market," the attorney says. "That is the owners intentions as of now."

"Definitely, so we're to focus on new flooring for the entire home, fresh paint throughout, updating all five bathrooms, and a complete demo of the kitchen?" Ridge confirms.

"Yes. Should you have any questions, here's my card. I know you'll need input on colors, and styles and I'll be coordinating with the family."

"Are they here?" I ask, my voice gruff. "The family?"

Ridge nods. "Yes, will anyone be staying here while we're working?"

"Yes, the owner is here, and they will be the point person for this project. She will be the one to direct questions or concerns to. You can also contact me if the family is unavailable. The family will be staying here in the home while you're renovating."

"Sounds great. Thank you." Ridge thrusts his hand out for a shake, and just like that, we get to work.

Stepping outside into the frigid January air, I take in a deep breath. The cool crisp air burns my lungs. I should feel relieved and I do, but I also feel disappointment seep into my bones. I wanted to walk into this house and see her. What I wouldn't give to see her again. My heart skips a beat at the thought of her being here, but I can't be that lucky. I'm sure it's her mother. I can't imagine that woman willingly giving up any kind of control. I've thought about seeing her again more times than I can count and each time, I imagine the two of us together, happily ever after and all that. However, I know I fucked up and that will never be. I just hope that during all this, that Delaney is the one who comes to represent the family, not her mother. Even though she might not accept it, I need to apologize to her. Tell her how I messed up and how she's all I wanted. Hell, she's still all I want. More and more each day as I watch the guys settle down, I think about her and what could have been.

"Yo, grab the other end of this," Tyler says, pulling my attention back to the present. He's got one end of the large tool chest. It's on wheels and makes packing tools in and out of jobsites so much easier, but the damn thing is heavy as hell and takes two guys to get it in and out of the truck.

Without a word, we carry the chest inside and get to work on the demo of the master bathroom. Ridge decided to start there to give the family member a suite of her own while we work. That is until it's time for flooring and paint. That all comes last. I'm lost in my head for the rest of the morning. The guys seem to understand that I'm trying to work something out because they leave me alone for the most part. Although they won't stay quiet forever. Especially when their wives find out. That's both the blessing and the curse of our tight-knit group.

It's just past one, and we're back at the jobsite after a quick lunch at the local diner in town. I expected questions from the guys, but all I got was an "Are you good?" from Ridge once we were seated. I answered him honestly with a "No, but I will be." I've learned from my past and know what not to do in the future.

"I'm heading out for the day, but I wanted to introduce you to the homeowner," Mr. Garcia says. "Oh, Ms. Nottingham," he says, looking behind us. I freeze. My heart stalls in my chest. I want to turn, but I can't seem to make my feet move. He said Ms., not Mrs. Is that because Mr. Nottingham passed? No, it can't be. It has to be her. She was an only child in this big, lonely house.

"Hello, Mr. Garcia," a smooth sexy voice answers.

It's her. It's Delaney. I would know that sweet voice anywhere. Swallowing hard, I turn to face her. She doesn't make eye contact with any of us; her eyes are on her attorney. "This is the construction company that's going to be updating the estate."

"Ridge Beckett." Ridge steps around us and offers her his hand.

I hate it. He's touching her and I'm not. What's worse is I should have been the one to introduce them. She's my girl, and I never did let them meet, and I should have and I hate myself for it. I hate that I kept her a secret.

"Delaney," I croak. The room falls silent and her attention turns to me.

She tilts her head to the side. "I'm sorry. Do I know you?" Her eyebrows are furrowed as if she's concentrating really hard to decide if she knows me.

What. The. Fuck?

"Really, Delaney?" I ask, not bothering to hide the frustration in my voice. Damnit, I don't want to be a dick to her, but pretending not to know me? Really?

"I'm sorry," she starts, but her attorney jumps in.

"As I was saying, Ms. Nottingham will be the point person. If she is unavailable, by all means, contact me," he says again. "Any questions, I will pass them on to Ms. Nottingham."

"Can we talk?" I ask her, ignoring him. My hands are fisted at my sides, fighting off the urge to pull her into my arms. It's been too damn long. I take one small step toward her.

"I'm sorry. I need to go," she says, backing away before turning and rushing down the hall.

I move to go after her, but Tyler places a hand on my shoulder, stopping me. "Not now," he says, low enough for only me to hear. I try to shake him off, but his grip is firm. It's probably better this way. I need to calm the hell down.

Dutifully, I stand still while Ridge and Mr. Garcia finish their conversation.

"Any questions?" Mr. Garcia asks.

"No, sir. We'll let you know if we run into any issues, and will seek guidance from Ms. Nottingham on the look she wants. The flooring will be replaced last in order to keep it free of damage during the construction phase," Ridge explains.

"That's quite all right. We'll provide you with weekly draws for payment every Friday."

"That's great. Thank you." Ridge shakes his hand and turns toward us. I feel a heavy hand on each shoulder as Mark and Tyler flank me, while Mr. Garcia moves around us and out the front door.

"What the fuck was that?" Ridge asks.

"Nothing." I shrug Mark and Tyler off me.

"That wasn't nothing," Seth says.

"Fine. We hooked up." It's wrong that I'm demeaning what she means to me, but fuck, she acted like she didn't even know who I was.

"And?" Ridge asks.

"And nothing. She wants to play games, I'm done."

"How long ago?" Tyler asks.

"Five years. Right before we went out of town when Ridge met Melissa."

They all nod. "And she's got you all worked up?"

"I'm not worked up."

"Right." Mark laughs.

"Fuck off," I grumble.

"You need me to put you on another job? Maybe have you hang out at the shop with Mara. I'm sure there are things for you to do."

"Hey, now, if anyone should get to hang out with my wife, it's me," Seth intervenes.

"You think I'm crazy? Putting any of us with our wives is a mistake if I want any work to get done." The four of them nod, knowing damn well Ridge is right.

"No. I'm fine. I'm over it."

"Sure, you are," Mark says, shaking his head.

"I'm good. Let's get this over with. The faster we get this job finished, the sooner I'm out of here."

"Kent, you do realize we're going to be here for several weeks, right?" Ridge asks.

"The longer we stand out here cackling like a bunch of hens, the longer it's going to take." I stalk off toward the master bedroom, all the while hoping I see her on the way. The guys don't push me for more; instead, they follow me down that hall, and we get to work.

I can't believe she acted like she didn't know me. After all the time we spent together. I've thought about how things would go if I ever ran into her again. This was not what I envisioned for our reunion. I didn't expect her to be pining over me, but damn, pretending she doesn't know me, that's harsh. This is going to be a long-ass job. The sooner we get out of there, the better. Even as I think the words, I'm also trying to decide how I can get her alone. How I can convince her to talk to me. Regardless of how she feels about me now, I need to apologize for how I acted back then. She also needs to know what she meant to me. What she still means to me. Something tells me none of that is going to go as easy as I had anticipated.

Chapter 3

Delaney

I rush down the hall to my bedroom and slam the door. I hate it when this happens. You would think that by now I'd be used to it—running into people from my past. As I rest my back against the door, I focus on taking in slow, even breaths. I hear their deep voices carry up the stairs and I resolve to hang out here in my room the rest of the day. It's not like I have anything pressing to do. Mom won't be here until the end of the week. I still can't seem to comprehend why she hates this place. This house is gorgeous, and it's huge. So much bigger than our home back in California. Then again, a house this size in Cali would be a considerable amount of money. We do well, but not that well. My dad was an architect, just like my grandfather.

My grandad actually designed and built this house on his own. When he passed, we moved here from a few towns over. Now, with Dad gone, Mom wants me to sell it. Maybe with the renovations, I can convince her that keeping it is a good idea. Then again, I'm an adult, and I don't need her permission. When I left California, I was in the mindset that selling it, even though Grandad built it, would be the best bet. Our life was hundreds of miles away. However, the more time I spend here, the more that just doesn't feel right to me.

Having caught my breath, I move to the bed and stare up at the ceiling. I want to stay holed up in here all day, but I know I can't do that. I can't hide from the gorgeous man covered in ink. I need to face him. He's hauntingly familiar, so much so that I see him in my dreams.

Literally.

I've dreamed about him many times over the years. I don't know what that means exactly, but with the way those dark eyes of his were staring at me, the look of disbelief on his face, I know for certain it's only a matter of time before I find out.

I will face him eventually. For now, I'm going to finish this book I'm reading. It's a new one from Evan Grace, and I have to know what happens. Grabbing my Kindle from the nightstand, I immerse myself into another world. Reading is my escape from life, from reality. When life gets blurry or messy, I can always depend on my favorite authors to give me a few hours of reprieve from reality.

Two hours pass, and I have a smile on my face. The ending was perfect. As I close my Kindle, my stomach growls loudly, reminding me I didn't eat this morning. Steeling my resolve, it's time to head downstairs. If I'm lucky, I won't run into them. Quietly, I open the bedroom door and peer both ways down the hall. I hear them working downstairs, but it's hard to tell which room they're in. Slowly, I take one step at a time. As I grow closer, I hear they're in the master bedroom, which just so happens to be the only downstairs bedroom. Perfect.

Making my way to the kitchen, I pull out a loaf of bread and a jar of peanut butter and a container of honey. I'm just about ready to take my first bite when I hear footsteps enter the kitchen. I don't have to turn around to know it's him. I can feel it, which is an odd sensation. My skin prickles and what feels like hundreds of butterflies take flight in my still empty stomach.

"Delaney." His deep voice surrounds me.

Might as well get this over with. Leaving my sandwich on the paper towel, I turn to face him. His dark eyes stare at me intently. Neither one of us says a word while we survey the other. He's tall, well over six-foot, ink-black hair, tattoos peeking out everywhere, and dark eyes. He's

24

gorgeous in that bad boy kind of way. He looks like trouble, but when I peer into his eyes, it's as if I can see into his soul, and they tell a different story. His dark orbs tell me that seeing me hurts him.

"Hi." I wave awkwardly. My voice is high-pitched, my nerves getting the best of me. He's very intimidating.

"What was that about earlier?" he asks.

"What do you mean?" I know exactly what he means, and I've been down this road before; it's just not one I like to travel.

"Pretending not to know who I am." He winces as if saying those words causes him pain.

Taking a deep breath, I try to explain. "I'm sorry. I don't know you; at least, I don't remember you."

"Fuck," he murmurs, running his hands through that thick black hair. My eyes take in the ink on his hands. I wish the sleeves of his shirt didn't hide his arms, so I could see more of the intricate work.

I hate this part. "Look, this is never easy." I pause, wringing my hands together, preparing to tell the story all over again. I hate the looks of pity I get after I tell my truth. I don't want to see sympathy in his eyes, but I know it's coming. "A few years ago, I was in a car accident. I lost my memory. I've had to learn my family, my friends, everything all over again. I'm sorry that I don't remember you. Were we friends?" I ask softly.

His eyes rake over my body. "Accident?" he asks. "D-Do you remember anything?"

"Yes and no. I have flashbacks sometimes, just these small glimpses of scenes that I'm in. I assume they're memories. You're in them," I confess. He's been a recurring role in my dreams. When I ask my mother who he is, she says she doesn't recall. Something tells me he was important to me. Especially if the look he's giving me is any indication.

"Were you hurt?" He takes a step forward and lifts his hand only to drop it at his side and form a fist. "Of course you were. You lost your memory, but I mean, are you okay?" His expressive eyes tell me he's not asking to be nosey or gossip; he cares. He truly cares if I'm hurting, or that I was at one time. There is no pity in his gaze. Just concern and something else I can't quite name.

"I was in a coma for a few days, well, fourteen to be exact; at least, that's what they tell me. I had some bumps and bruises, a broken arm, but the worst of it was the memory loss. I hit my head pretty hard."

I watch him closely as he swallows hard. "Will you ever get it back?"

I shrug. "The doctors are optimistic. I've remembered a few things over the years, all from my early childhood. And then there's this place." I tear my gaze from his and let my eyes wander around the room. "This is my first time here since the accident, but it's so familiar to me in ways. I FaceTimed with my mom last night, and she said the room I chose to sleep in is the room I stayed in when we lived here. My mind does that. Guides me to who I once was without reminding me of the time or place. It can be overwhelming." I don't know why I'm telling him all of this. My only excuse is that he genuinely looks pained for me—or for him. I'm not so sure.

"You dreamed about me?" he asks, his voice softer.

I nod. "Yeah, but when I described you, no one in my family could tell me who you were. How did we know each other?"

"We were together. I mean, we dated when you were home from college on break."

No. It can't be. My body stiffens immediately. I let my eyes roam over him yet again, and all the similarities smack me in the face. It's him. I don't know why I didn't notice before now. I can only assume my avoidance had something to do with it. My mother didn't warn me he was from Jackson, or of the chance that he might still be here.

"What's wrong?" He takes another step closer. His hand reaches for me, but I take a step back, hitting the counter.

"Stop." I hold my hands up to keep him from moving toward me any further. "You threw me away." I hate the emotion I hear in my voice. I can't remember the incident, but I know what my mother told me. Not a day has gone by that I haven't thought about the man who didn't want me. The one who tossed me to the side, not bothering to come to the hospital to see me. How could he be so callous? From the look in his eyes, I meant something to him. Then again, maybe that's just my mind playing tricks on me. I want to believe I was more to him, but the truth is in his actions. He never showed up. All these years later, he never tried to find me or come visit.

"No." He takes another step and then another until we're standing toe-to-toe. My hands press against his rock-hard chest, trying to maintain some type of distance between us. "I made a mistake, but I never threw you away, Delaney. I tried to call you. You wouldn't answer your phone or return my messages. I came here to see you, and your mother said you'd found someone else, that you were moving in with him and moving on. Without me," he grits out. His dark brown eyes plead with me to believe him. Is he an actor?

"What? That's absurd. Why would she tell you that?" I try to think back to the conversations we've had about him. She told me he didn't want me. She said that he told me to leave and never come back. That's what caused my accident. I was upset and driving. I couldn't see through the tears and my broken heart. That's what my mother told me. Why is he lying to me?

"Delaney." He lifts his calloused hand to my cheek and cradles it. "I promise you, I didn't throw you away. I made a mistake our last night together. I showed up, but I was a few hours late. I was wrong to keep you waiting."

"What do you mean?" My voice cracks as the words form on my lips.

"I was supposed to meet you, Laney. You were headed back to college the next day, and it was our last night together. You said you had something you wanted to talk to me about and I chickened out. I wasn't ready to face my feelings for you."

"Your feelings?" I whisper.

He nods, swallows hard, and his next words stall my heart in my chest. "I was in love with you."

"Sorry to interrupt," the tall guy with longer hair says. "We need some help hauling this out to the trailer."

"I'll be there in a minute," the man before me tells him. He doesn't once pull his eyes away from me.

I realize I don't know his name. We have all this history. History I don't remember. History that has only been filled in bit by bit from my mother. History that, from the look in his eyes, I know nothing about. Is he telling the truth? His story and Mom's don't add up, but the look in his eyes, it's clear he believes with everything in him that what he says is true. I can see and feel it coming off him in waves. "What's your name?"

"Kent, well, Kenton is my full name." He runs his thumb across my cheek as my heart races. "You would call me Kenton if you were mad at me." He smiles softly, the gesture lighting up his face.

"Oh my God," I whisper.

"What?" His shoulders stiffen, but his dark eyes still bore into mine.

"That's why she hated it."

"Who hated what, baby?" His tone is soft, dare I say loving? It's unexpected, but not unwelcome. The way he looks at me, the reverence in his voice, I can feel it deep inside that I was important to him. That he was important to me. I just wish I could remember.

"My mother. She hated the name, but it was my choice. The one thing I could control. I didn't let her stop me."

"Delaney, what name? What are you talking about?"

I swallow hard as I prepare to drop a bomb on him. I'm sure he assumes with the accident that things worked out how he wanted them to. Then again, if what he's saying is true. He doesn't know. I don't know what to believe, but I do know it's him. I might not fully remember, but I see him in my dreams, and she's his spitting image. "My daughter. My mother hates her name. To this day, she still complains."

"Your daughter?" he asks, swallowing hard.

I nod.

"What's her name, Delaney?" The hand that's not cupping my cheek grips my hip, tethering me to him.

"Kendrix. Her name is Kendrix."

He nods. "How old is she?"

"She'll be five in March." I watch as he processes what I'm telling him. "She looks like you."

His face goes pale. Even behind his beard, I can see it. "Is she mine?"

I shrug. "I don't know." I hate that I can't remember. What I do know is that the similarities between the two are uncanny.

"C-Can I see her? I mean, do you have a picture of her?" His gaze penetrates mine as he swallows hard, waiting for my reply. His jaw is still, and his eyes dark—almost black with the storm of emotions raging inside him.

I can see it. He's worked the time out in his head. He knows as well as I do that my daughter is also his. I just wish I could remember. And what about my mom? The story she told me is nothing like what this handsome stranger—well, I guess he's not a stranger—is telling me. Is he lying? Did she lie to me? I don't know. I don't see the harm in showing him her picture. It will get a reaction out of him. He can see what I see and we'll have to take it from there. I'm used to that. My life is one big "we'll take it from here." I hate there are these huge missing pieces of my past that I can't put together. Maybe Kenton will be my missing piece? Maybe he can help me remember?

Nodding, I reach for my phone in my back pocket. Unlocking the screen, I scroll through my pictures until I find one of just her and me. Turning the phone toward him, I show him the picture of Kendrix and me the day I left to come here. "She's with my mom. She convinced me to let her stay with her so I could get everything on track with the attorney and the construction crew. Well, you." I offer him a smile. My mother was adamant that Kendrix stayed with her, and it wasn't worth the fight. I didn't know the condition of the house. But to hear Mom tell it, it was in dire straits. I wanted to check it out before I brought my daughter here. Is this why, though? The real reason? Was she afraid Kenton would see her? That he would recognize himself in her?

"She has your eyes," he says, not tearing away from the image on the screen. "Big blue eyes just like her mamma."

"And black hair," I state the obvious. "A trait she had to have gotten from her father."

"Yo, Kent, let's go!" one of the guys yells out.

He sighs heavily. "We need to talk. I have so many questions. I don't know what this means, but she looks like me. Like us. If I'm her father, I want to be in her life. I just—Have dinner with me tonight?" He pulls his eyes from my phone to look at me. "I feel it deep in here"—he taps my hand that is still resting on his chest over his heart—"that she's mine, Laney." He shortens my name and it sparks something inside me. No one calls me Laney, yet it's so familiar. I get this feeling of déjà vu every time he does it. "I want her. I want both of you. I know you don't remember us, but I do. We have to talk about this." His voice is pleading and stern at the same time.

He's not going to back down and honestly, I don't want him to. I can't explain it, but I feel connected to him, and not just because my body is plastered against his. It's more than that.

Deeper.

"Okay." I don't even hesitate. Something tells me that this man is a huge missing link to my life, to my daughter's life. I want to hear his side. I have my mother's side, her version of what happened before my accident. Now I want his. I can only hope that eventually, it will all come back to me, and I will learn the truth. Although, something tells me Kenton is a straight shooter. I feel as though I can trust him. But... I can trust my mother too, right? At least one would think so. I do remember growing up, everything until college, and my mom has always been a control freak. That's a memory that just came back a few months ago, but this isn't something I would put past her. I didn't have a choice but to believe her. I didn't have a name or a location or anything else to go off of.

"I'll pick you up at seven."

"Okay," I say again, because what else is there to say? From the look on his face, he didn't know about me being pregnant, if he is actually the father, but there are too many similarities for him not to be. Not to mention, something in my gut tells me he is. I've learned to trust that instinct since I don't have the memories to back me up.

He takes me by surprise when he leans in and presses a tender kiss to my forehead. Stepping back, his thumbs fly across the screen of my phone before he hands it back to me. "I added my number and texted myself that picture." He looks down at the floor for three heartbeats exactly. I know because I counted before he looks up under long lashes at me. "She's mine, Delaney. I can feel it. I want—" He stops and swallows hard. "I'll pick you up at seven." Giving my hip a gentle squeeze, he drops his hand and steps back. He walks backward for several steps before turning and walking out the door.

I was dreading facing him, explaining the story of my accident yet again. It's the same story I've had to tell more times than I can count over the years. However, this time, this time the story had a different ending. One that's muddled with what I see in his eyes and the conviction in his voice, versus what I've always been told. The two are fighting against one another like oil and water.

I'm glad we're getting together tonight. I have so many unanswered questions, as I'm sure he does as well. I debate on calling my mother and calling her out on all of this, but I fight it. I'm going to wait and see how tonight goes. Hear his side of things and try to piece them together. Seems like that's all I've been doing these last five years—piecing small bits of information—yet nothing seems complete. At least it didn't. Awareness rushes through me. This trip might be more than just overseeing renovations. Maybe I'll find my past and combine it with my future.

What are the odds?

Chapter 4

KENT

The rest of the day, I walk around in a haze. The guys pretty much leave me alone and let me work out all this shit bouncing around in my head. I look for her around every corner and have to fight with myself to not go in search of her. I've pulled my phone out of my pocket and looked at the picture of her daughter what feels like a thousand times.

That last night, the night I stood her up when she wanted to talk to me, I thought she wanted more, but maybe it was more than I ever could have imagined. Maybe she was going to tell me she was pregnant. That I was going to be a father. Her daughter looks like me, but with Delaney's blue eyes. I've been over it and over it in my mind, and the timeline fits. She's mine. I feel it deep in my bones. This little girl is my daughter. A daughter I've been away from the last almost five years, a daughter I never knew about, who doesn't know me.

I fucking hate it.

Tossing my tools into one of the crates, I wince at the noise. I've been tossing things around all day, being rougher than I should, but I'm mad. I'm beyond mad. I'm pissed, livid, infuriated, and I don't know what to think about all of this. If what she told me is true, she doesn't remember me. And I believe her. The connection we had, even though I refused to name it at the time, was intense, and no way could she hide that I know her intimately. Every inch of her body has been caressed by my hands, by my tongue. The time we spent together is not something that you can fake not remembering.

Another swarm of anger courses through me. She was hurt, in a hospital bed, and I wasn't with her. I would have been there. Sure, I was an idiot, but if she needed me, if I had known, I would have been by her side every step of the way.

And the baby… I missed it all. I missed Delaney growing round with my child, watching her body change, being there the moment Kendrix took her first breath. Those are moments I'll never get back.

"What did that hammer do to you?" Tyler asks.

I glare at him because I'm not in the mood for their shit. I need to get out of this house, get home, shower, and come back to pick her up. Hell, I'm tempted to have her ride to the shop with me to get my truck and take her straight to my place. The only thing stopping me is that she deserves better. She might not remember that night, the night I stood her up, but I do. I'm no longer that guy, and I'll show her what she means to me, even if she can't remember. Maybe one day she will and she'll know I've changed. I'm no longer afraid of what I feel for her. Hell, I don't even really know what that is.

Not this new version of her.

"We done here?" I ask him.

"Yeah, this is the last box." He lifts it into his arms and walks out the door.

Before I can stop myself, I jog to the kitchen. I saw her go in there about an hour ago and I've been watching for her to come back out. I stand in the doorway and watch as she dips out cookie dough onto a baking sheet. "We're heading out," I say, taking a step into the room.

"Oh, um, thanks." She looks down at the scoop in her hands then back up at me and grins. "I felt like baking."

"I can see that. I'll be back at seven, maybe a little before."

"Great. Sure, that's great," she says, and I see her nerves shining through. I'm glad to know I'm not the only one.

"I'll be here." My voice holds conviction. She doesn't realize that the last time I promised her I would be somewhere, I flaked out on her. Not this time. Never again in fact.

"I'll be ready." A slight blush coats her cheeks, and I have to force my feet to stay rooted to where I'm standing when all I really want to do is kiss the hell out of her. It's been too long since I've had my lips on hers. I know that's my own fault. But in a way, I wonder what would have happened if I had shown up that night. Would she still have been in that accident? Would her mom still have fed me some bullshit line about her moving on? Would I have so easily accepted that as our fate? I'd like to think not, but we can't change the past.

"See you soon." My voice is husky as I force myself to turn and leave her standing looking sexy as hell in her kitchen.

"What's up, Kent?" Ridge asks. He and I are in his truck, while Seth, Mark, and Tyler are in the other company truck.

"She has a kid."

"Yours?"

"The timeline fits."

"What does she say about it?"

"It's fucked up, man. She was in an accident and has amnesia or some shit. It's almost too fucking crazy to be real, but I know her, and she can't fake this. We were too close for too long."

"Why didn't you ever talk about her?"

"I was an idiot," I mumble, turning to look out the window. There is no other reason or excuse other than I was a complete idiot. I didn't realize what I had until she was gone. No, that's not true. I knew what I had, but I was too chicken shit to admit my feelings. I fucked up, plain and simple.

"There's more to this story."

I nod. "Yeah, but I'm processing. Hell, I'm not even sure I know the half of it. I'm picking her up at seven and taking her back to my place so we can talk."

"Anything I can do?" he asks.

"No. I have to deal with this shit, and we have to work it out on our own. I don't know where to even start." My phone vibrates in my pocket. Pulling it out, I see a message from my mom asking me if I want to come over for dinner.

Me: Sorry, have plans. This weekend?

Mom: Sure. Dad says hi.

Me: Tell him hi. Love you.

I close out of her message, not waiting for her reply, and see the one right below it. The one I sent myself from Delaney's phone. "Actually," I say to Ridge as we pull into the shop parking lot. "Take a look." I open the message and hold the phone up for him.

He stares at it for a long time, before his eyes move away from the phone to focus on me. "Congratulations, brother. She looks just like you."

"The eyes. She has Delaney's eyes."

"You're going to still test to make sure, right?" he asks.

"Yeah, I mean, we have to at this point. She can't remember our time together, but I do." I remember every damn second. "I need to prove it to both of us, and if she is mine, which I think she is, the timeline just fits, I want to get to know her."

"We've got your back. Whatever you need."

"Thanks. I haven't told the guys. Can we just… keep this between us at least until after tonight? She and I need to talk about this. We barely touched the surface earlier, and my brain is a jumbled mess. There is so much that's happened. It doesn't seem real."

"Sure thing," he answers just as Seth knocks on his window, making a goofy face and laughing as he jogs to his truck to start it. "How does Mara put up with him?" Ridge asks, laughing.

"She's a saint." With that, I head to my own truck to rush home and get ready.

"Come on in and have a seat." I push open the front door to my condo and hold it open for her. "Make yourself at home," I say, taking her coat and hanging both hers and mine on the hook just by the door.

"It's nice."

"You've been here before," I tell her.

"I have?" Her brow furrows as if she's trying to recall the memory.

"Yeah, we used to spend a lot of time here together."

"I'm sorry. I wish I could remember."

Damn, that cuts to the bone. "Let's start at the beginning. Tell me everything."

"I don't know you."

I nod. "I know you don't remember me, but we were close. Really close, and, Delaney, I'm pretty sure that your daughter is our daughter. I think Kendrix is mine. I've run the dates in my head a thousand times today. The timeline fits."

"We were sleeping together?" she asks.

"Yeah, we had been for a couple of years."

She scoots closer to her end of the couch, away from me. "Why should I believe you?"

I rack my brain for some kind of proof, of some sort of evidence I can show her, and that's when it hits me. Pulling my phone out of my pocket, I scroll to the one photo I allowed myself to keep all these years. "This," I say, handing her my phone. "This photo was taken the day before you left for college after your break. I was supposed to meet you later that night. We got a room at a bed and breakfast. We didn't need to because we had my place, but you said it would be romantic. I agreed. We took this picture then. That was the last time I saw you."

"My accident, it was in California." I can hear the confusion in her voice as she tries to piece all of this, piece me into her life.

"Yeah." I swallow hard. "I was late. Really late, like over four hours. When I got to the bed and breakfast, you had already checked out."

"Why were you late?"

"I fucked up. I was reeling from what you made me feel. I was upset that you were going back to school. I was going to miss you and didn't know how to handle that."

"How long did we... date?"

37

"We weren't exclusive," I admit. I want to tell her that we were madly in love and that we should ride off into the sunset, but I have a feeling she's been lied to way too much these past few years. I will never be anything but honest with her. "For about two years, every time you came home for break or for the summer, we were together."

"But we weren't official? We weren't dating?"

"No."

"Did you want to?"

"Yes. However, at the time I didn't admit that to you or myself."

"What did we do? When we were together?"

"Movies, dinner. We spent a lot of time out at the lake just sitting in the back of my truck. Sleeping under the stars, skinny dipping a time or two." I smile, trying to lighten the mood, and the load I'm sure that's sitting on her shoulders, just as it is mine. This is a lot to process.

"We were sleeping together?"

"Yes."

"How long?"

"From the night we first met." She nods, accepting my answer. This has to be hard for her. I wait patiently, giving her time to catalogue what I've said.

"How did we meet?"

"I was with the guys at Bottom's Up. That's a local bar here in town. You were home on summer break. Something I learned you did every year. It was the summer before your third year of college. I don't know how I missed seeing you before then. The moment I laid eyes on you, I knew you were someone I wanted to spend time with."

"So, you wanted to sleep with me?" The corner of her mouth tilts into a grin.

"Yes."

"You're being very… honest and open about all of this. I don't sense you trying to sway me in any one direction."

"I will always be honest and open with you. I have nothing to hide. I've regretted that last night, the one I was late for, since the moment I found out you had checked out of the B&B. I wasn't honest with you or myself until it was too late. I vowed to never be that guy again."

"So… we slept together that first night? Sorry, I know that's what you said, but that's not me. Not the me I am now. I just… I'm trying to wrap my head around all of this."

"Yes. However, I'd also like to note that we were both drinking, but neither one of us were too drunk that we couldn't make an informed decision about what we were doing. Our chemistry was palpable."

"And after that?"

"You were home for a week. We spent any time I wasn't at work together until you went back to school. We texted here and there, and then when you came home for spring break, you called me. We met up, and the cycle began."

"We were dating, but not dating." She laughs and my shoulders relax.

"Pretty much. We never talked about it. We didn't label it. We were just… us."

"You said you came to see me. When?"

"I tried calling you for a few weeks. Calling, sending text messages, but you didn't reply. I went to your parents' place to ask for your address at school. I was coming to you. I couldn't stand the silence. I couldn't stand the fact that you thought I didn't want you. It was my fault. I let my worries and my fear keep me from you, and then you were gone back to school." I go on to tell her the conversation I had with her mom about her moving on and moving in with her new boyfriend. "It wasn't two weeks later the moving trucks rolled in and your parents moved away. It was… I assumed from what your mother told me, to be closer to you and your fiancé." I'll never forget that day and the way her mother's words affected me. As if I'd been punched in the gut.

"This is a lot to take in. I have you sitting here showing me this picture and answering questions without hesitation, and then I have the version of what my mother told me about you and our relationship." She closes her eyes and takes a deep breath. "I think we should have a paternity test done, but I'm pretty sure I know what the results are going to be. Kendrix looks just like you."

"Except for your baby blues," I say softly. "She's mine," I say with conviction. "I can feel it, Delaney." She smiles gently, and I can't imagine what she's been going through, thinking I didn't want her. "What did they tell you? About me?"

"How much time do you have?"

"All night. I have some chili in the Crock-Pot. Are you hungry?"

"Is that what smells so good? It smells amazing."

"Come on, let's get you fed, and you can tell me your story." Standing, I hold my hand out for her and she doesn't hesitate to take it, allowing me to help her stand from her corner of the couch. Not willing to let her go just yet, I place my hand on the small of her back and lead her to the kitchen. She takes a seat at the small table, and I commit the image to memory. It's been too long since she's been here. Not just in my condo, but in this town. I just hope I can convince her to stay. If not, I have a big choice to make. I don't want to miss anymore time with my daughter.

Chapter 5

Delaney

Sitting across from Kent at his small kitchen table, I feel more at home than I have ever been. I don't remember this place, so it must be him. About six months after my accident, I started to see him in my dreams. We never spoke, but he was always there, offering me his hand, trying to get me to come with him. To follow him. I always wake up before I see where he wants me to go. It's frustrating as hell.

"So…," he says, letting that one word hang between us. We're strangers, yet from our conversation earlier, we're not. It's all very overwhelming.

"My accident happened when I was driving back to school; at least, that's what they tell me. I was in a coma for two weeks, and when I woke up, the doctor informed me that I was pregnant. I didn't know my family. I didn't know anyone. I had no recollection of my life before that day."

"I can't begin to imagine what that felt like."

"Scary, overwhelming. I was lost and defeated. My parents brought in photo albums and told me stories, but it was like I was talking to strangers."

"Did you ever remember them?"

"Yeah, about a month after the accident, I woke up and it was like a lightbulb came on inside my head. I remember everything up to my high school graduation. After that, those years are lost."

"Do they know why?" he asks.

"The doctors have a theory." I'm biding my time. Kent seems like a great guy, and what I say next will hurt him if my suspicions are correct. However, I owe him the same honesty that he's given me.

"Is that something you can share with me?"

"I can." I nod. "I'm just not sure that I should."

"You can trust me, Delaney." The deep timbre of his voice seeps into my soul, and I can just feel that the words he speaks are true.

"It's not about trust. I don't want to hurt you."

"I'm a big boy. I can take it."

"The doctors think that I'm suppressing the memories because they're too painful."

"Is that what you think?"

"Before today, yeah, I did." They had me convinced, and I didn't know otherwise.

"And now?"

"Now, I'm not so sure. Now I feel as though they, meaning my parents, toyed with me. They made me believe the version they wanted." It was more my mother, but my father stayed silent on the matter. He's guilty by association. He's gone, and I hate that I'll never get to ask him why.

"What did they tell you?"

"When the doctor told me I was pregnant, and it was obvious that my memory was gone, Mom told me that you left me. That I told you about the baby and you told me to end it and that you never wanted to see me again. Well, I say you, but my 'man friend' is how she referred to you. She refused to give me your name and told me I was better off without your hatred in my life."

"I didn't know. I promise you, if I had known, I wouldn't have stopped until I found you." Resting his elbows on the table, he runs his hands over his face. "I shouldn't have taken her word for it. I knew she hated me, but when you didn't reply to any of my calls or messages, I thought that's what you wanted."

"I don't know. I don't know what I would have wanted. I'm... confused. I don't know why my mother would do this."

"Earlier, you said she hated the name Kendrix?"

"Yes. She was pissed at me for weeks. She still refuses to call her that. It's always Grandma's girl or something. She rarely uses her given name unless she's scolding her."

"Kendrix, Kenton, they have a nice ring to them," he says, giving me a smile.

I appreciate that he's trying to lighten the mood with all the heavy that surrounds us. "They have similarities," I agree with him. "Look, I don't know you, and I'm sorry I don't remember our time together. If you are her father, I won't keep her from you."

"I'm her father."

"How are you so certain? Dark hair and similar facial features could just be a coincidence."

"It's not. You told me you had something to tell me that night. I was afraid you were going to tell me that you were in love with me. I didn't know what to say. I only wanted you, but I'd never said those words to a woman, unless you count my mom. I was scared of what I felt for you and I didn't face it. I was leaving to meet you when the guys called asking me to meet up for a beer. I went there first. I sat at the table nursing a beer all night, my mind constantly on you. I'm sorry about that. I should have been there for you. I made you think you weren't important to me, and that's not what it was. I was an idiot."

"I wouldn't know." I shrug as if I'm letting his words bounce off my shoulders. The truth is, the sincerity of his words penetrates my soul. After thinking for years he had cast me aside, it's nice to sit face-to-face and learn that wasn't the case at all. He loved me.

"I want to be in her life. I want to hear about your pregnancy and delivery. I want to know her first words and when she took her first steps. I want to know it all. I've missed so much."

"Don't you think we should have the test done first?"

"No. She's mine."

"I think we should have the test done before you meet her. She's going to be five in a couple of months. She's smart and picks up on things quickly. She's asked me already where her daddy is."

"W-What did you tell her?"

"That Daddy lived far away with his family and couldn't be with us." He gives me a "really" look. "I panicked. It's not like I wanted to tell her my mother's version of the story. I couldn't tell her that her father told me to end my pregnancy. I had to think of something. I didn't have my own memory, and I refused to make her think less of you. Not without me knowing, without me remembering the truth. That's all I could come up with when she put me on the spot." I always hoped my memory would come back. I would have my own version, my own words and memories to help make her understand.

"When can we do the test? I have five years to make up for."

"She and my mother are flying in on Thursday."

"What time?"

"Kent, I don't want you to meet her until the test is done."

"Schedule it," he says through gritted teeth. "I've missed enough time with her. In fact, I'll schedule it. What time does their flight land?"

"They should be here early afternoon."

He nods. "I'll look into having someone come to you. I don't want her scared by going to the hospital."

"Do they do that?"

"I don't know, but I'm going to find out."

"I'm sure it's expensive."

"Don't care."

We sit in silence. Our bowls of chili have long since been emptied, and I'm sure, like me, he's trying to wrap his head around today. It's been information overload. I don't know what to think or what to feel. My mother, I don't know why she would do this to me. Then there's my dad. He was always the quiet one. He never said much, but I do remember him standing up for me when Kendrix was born. My mom was angry, and when I say angry, not just "oh woe is me... I'm disappointed in you." She was pissed and didn't talk to me for three full days when I named my daughter.

"How long are you here for?"

"Just overseeing the renovations. However long that takes."

"And Kendrix?" he asks. I swear the way he says her name with reverence, it does something to me. It makes me want to believe him and everything he's said, but then there's my mother.

"She'll be here with me."

"Where's home to you? California?"

Home. Again, I'm hit with the fact that I feel more at home here in his kitchen than I have since the day I woke up after the accident. I'm not even going to think about why that might be. "Yeah."

"You selling once the reno is done? Have you thought about maybe sticking around? Making Tennessee home?"

"I think we're jumping the gun just a little, don't you think? I mean, come on. You have a theory that since we were sleeping together, that my daughter is yours. I don't know you. You could be making all of this up. There will be no discussions of moving or visitation or anything else related to my daughter until your theory is proven." I wait for him to balk and back down, but he does the opposite.

"Good. I'll pay them to put a rush on the results. I refuse to lose anymore time with her." He stands and takes both our empty bowls to the sink and rinses them off. I watch his muscles flex under his tight-fitting long-sleeved T-shirt while he loads them into the dishwasher. When he's finished his task, he turns and leans against the counter, crossing his ankles and his arms across his broad chest. "There will be visitations, and one of us is going to have to move. I will not lose anymore time with her." His voice is stern and his jaw is set.

He really believes he's her father. "I'm ready to go home now." I stand and push in my chair, taking my glass to the sink. "Thank you for having me." Turning, I walk toward the living room, slide into my boots and coat, and wait for him to join me.

The ride home is silent and filled with tension. The few times I glanced at Kent, I could see the white of his knuckles from the lights on the dash of his truck. His jaw is set, and I'm sure his mind is racing as he tries to process today. I know mine is.

45

He pulls up to the front door in the circular drive, and I reach for the door handle. His hand on my arm stops it. Then again, maybe it's his gravelly voice as he says my name.

"Delaney."

I freeze as my eyes find his in the dimly lit cab. "I'm sorry."

"No." His voice is gruff as he shakes his head. "You have nothing to be sorry for. I should have been there. That night. I promised you I was going to meet you there and I wasn't. This is all on me." He swallows hard, his dark eyes boring into me. "I'm going to make it up to you. To both of you. I want you, both of you in my life. I know you don't remember me." He stops as his hand moves from my arm to cradle my cheek, and I can't seem to stop my body's reaction to him as I lean into his touch. "I don't care where I have to go, or what I have to do. I'm going to be there. You hear me, Laney?" He leans in close and presses his forehead to mine. "I'm going to be there for both of you. No matter what."

"I should go." I pull away with great effort, and pull on the handle climbing out of the truck. By the time I manage to climb out and get my door shut, he's there, standing next to me. Hand on the small of my back, he walks me to the door.

"Thank you for letting me talk, to spend time with you. I'm calling first thing tomorrow for a lab. I'll let you know what I find out."

"How are you so certain? This is all so unexpected. I mean, come on, what are the odds that you, the man I see in my dreams, are the father of my daughter?"

"The odds are unexpected, but the best things in life are uncertain."

"How can you say that?"

"Because you're uncertain about me, about the paternity of our daughter, and I know that the two of you in my life will be the best thing that has ever happened to me." With that, he leans in and presses a kiss to my cheek. "Good night, Laney." Shoving his hands in his front pockets, he steps back and waits for me to be safely inside before jogging back to his truck.

I peek through the blinds and watch until I can no longer see his taillights. My hand touches my cheek where his lips just were, and I can still feel them, soft yet firm, pressed against my skin.

What I did tonight was dangerous and out of character for me. I allowed a strange man to pick me up and take me back to his place. I don't know him, even though in my gut, it feels like I do. It's not just my gut, but his eyes; they tell me more than anything that we meant something to each other. I need to call my mother. I need to confront her, but part of me wants to sit on this new information for a few days. Maybe, the more time I'm here, my memories will come back to me. Maybe I won't need my mother's story or Kenton's. I'll have my own.

Chapter 6

KENT

When my alarm finally sounds at 6:00 a.m., I've been awake for hours. I finally managed to fall asleep sometime after one in the morning, only to wake back up at two thirty. I've been lying here in bed ever since. I'm not tired. My mind is racing and I can't seem to shut it off.

She was here.

In my house.

She had my baby.

She can't remember me.

Never in my wildest dreams could I ever have imagined that this would be our outcome. That the woman I love, have loved for years, doesn't remember our time together. I knew that a part of me would always be hers, with how deeply she burrowed herself under my skin all those years ago. However, seeing her now, knowing what I know, knowing that her daughter is mine, it's clear to me that it's more than just a piece of me that's hers. It's all of me. Everything I am.

Rushing through a shower, and a pot of coffee later, I'm loaded up and heading to the shop. The lab doesn't open until eight, and that's about the time we'll get on the jobsite. I'll just have to step away to make the call. I'm not putting this off. I want the test and I want my daughter.

Pulling into the shop, I'm the last to arrive. Good, that's how I wanted this to go down. Less time for idle chitchat. Instead of going inside, I hop into Ridge's truck just like yesterday. I've barely got the door shut before the guys come filing out of the office. Seth is last, of course, just like always. Not that I can blame him. If Delaney worked here, I'd always be last too.

"Mornin'," Ridge says, climbing behind the wheel.

"I need to call the lab at eight." I blurt the words like a confession.

"Good plan." He puts the truck in Drive and pulls out of the lot, pointing us toward the Nottingham Estate. Pointing us toward Delaney.

"She's mine." I already told him this yesterday, but I need to say it again. Out loud to someone I know. It's almost as if I need to claim her, claim both of them publicly since my dumbass let that opportunity pass me by last time. Never again.

"How did last night go?"

"Fine." I run my fingers through my hair. "She came over, we had dinner, we talked. I told her my version of the story, and she told me the version her mother told her. Her mother never liked me. Never approved of us being together. It all makes sense. The timeline fits."

"And how does Delaney feel about all of this?"

"Fuck, man. Angry, confused. She doesn't know me, Ridge. She doesn't remember our time together. I had a picture of us, one we took the last time we were together. It's the only one I've ever allowed myself to keep of us, as a reminder. I showed it to her and could see the confusion and the disbelief in her eyes."

"I can imagine this is tough on her."

"On her, on me, on my daughter. Fuck, I have a daughter." A daughter who is close to Knox in age and I've never met. A daughter who thinks that family other than her is what has kept me away from her all these years. A daughter I've never held in my arms or tucked in bed at night.

"You can't push her, Kent. You know that, right? I know what you're feeling. I know you. You want her and your kid right now, all the time. I get it. I do. However, you can't push either of them. If her memory doesn't come back, she might not ever be yours."

"They're mine," I say through gritted teeth.

"Look, man. I know where you're coming from. I do. But she doesn't remember you, Kent. How can you expect her to just pick up where you left off when those memories are yours alone?"

I let his words sink in and he's right. No matter how much I want to pull her into my arms and never let go, I can't do that. Glimpses of me in her dreams isn't enough. What other choice do I have? "I'll make her remember," I answer my own question aloud. "I'll show her what we were together. I'll make her fall in love with me again."

"Again?" Ridge questions.

"Again. There is no doubt in my mind that she loved me. I ran from it. Worried about settling down. Fuck me, I was a dick. I should have been there that night. She had something to tell me, and my dumb ass thought she was going to tell me she loved me and that she wanted a commitment. What she didn't know was that I was already committed to her. I just never told her. There was no one else for me when she went back to school. It was always just her. Just Delaney. Now I'm sure she was also going to tell me about our daughter. Did I tell you her name?" I ask him. "Kendrix." I don't give him the chance to reply. "It's as if subconsciously she was naming our little girl after me. Even though her family tried to tell her I didn't want her, it was as if her heart knew the truth. That I wanted them both. I *want* them both." I'm quick to add.

"We're here," Ridge says as he pulls up to the house. I know my best friend and his words have double meaning. Sure, we're at the jobsite, but he also meant he and the guys are here for me. Hell, so are the wives and the littles. I have a huge support system and I have never been more grateful for them. I want Laney and Kendrix to meet them. I know my family will accept them with open arms and maybe, just maybe, I can convince them to stay. The alternative is me leaving, not something I ever wanted to do, but I'll do it for them. For my girls, I would do anything.

"I'll be right there," I tell Ridge, pulling my phone out of my pocket. I call the lab and schedule someone to be here Friday morning. I have to pay extra for a technician to come out, but I'm fine with that. I don't want my little girl to have to go to the hospital for this. I'm sure she's going to be confused and scared as it is. They have assured me, that it's as simple as swabbing the inside of both our cheeks and that they will run the tests as soon as they can. It could take up to a week for the results, but processing times are usually two to three days in their lab. I chose the right place. The sooner I have it on paper as proof for my girls, the better.

I sit in the truck until I get my email confirmation for Friday's appointment. As soon as it comes through, I'm out of the truck and stalking toward the front door. When I enter, I see Delaney standing next to the window. "Morning, Laney," I say softly.

"Hi. I-I wasn't sure that you were coming in." Her face blushes a light shade of pink.

"Were you watching for me?" I ask, taking a small step toward her.

She shrugs her reply as her cheeks grow a darker shade of pink. "Last night was a lot to take on."

I nod. "It was, but you want to know something?" I ask, taking another step and then another. I don't stop until I'm standing toe-to-toe with her. Her gaze falls to our feet, and that won't do. Gently, I place my index finger under her chin and lift her eyes to mine. "I still want you. Both of you."

"Kenton." She breathes my name, and my heart stammers in my chest. Fuck me, but I've missed her.

"I was calling the lab. They'll be here Friday morning at eight. They've assured me it's nothing more than a swab to her cheek."

She nods. "I researched it last night. I didn't want to put her through something that would make her frightened."

"I told them to ask for me. I'll explain that she doesn't know that I'm being tested as well. I don't want to scare her, but, Laney, I'm her father. It takes up to a week for the results, but we could have them as soon as a few days. When we get them back and you have your concrete proof, I want her to know who I am."

"I promised you I wouldn't keep you from her."

"And what about you?"

"W-What about me?"

52

"I want you both, Laney. I don't care what I have to do to make that happen."

She's quiet for a few minutes, those big blue eyes of her assessing me. When she finally speaks, her words are like a balm to my soul. "I-I dreamt about you last night. It was a dream I've never had before. We were in a meadow, and you were holding your hand out for me. Usually, it's you, and you're reaching for me, but I can never tell where we are, and I never reach for you. This time... this time, I placed my hand in yours before I woke up."

"I can take you there. We spent a lot of time in that little meadow. It was our spot. Your mother didn't approve of me, so the meadow and my condo were where we spent most of our time together."

"I hear what you're saying, and the conviction in your voice tells me it's your truth." *It's our truth.* "My mind is spinning with all this information. With this version of my life I know nothing about. I don't know. I don't know what to believe. I'm so confused about all of this. I-I need to talk to my mother."

I hate this. I hate this divide. I hate that she doesn't remember the time we spent together. The feel of my hands as they trace her skin. The feel of my lips as they press against hers. I hate that she doesn't remember waking up in the bed of my truck, nothing but the blanket wrapped around our naked bodies. There is not a moment, a single second that I spent with her, that is not ingrained in my memory.

"Right. Of course," I say, dropping my hand from her chin and taking a step back. "She'll be here Thursday, right? With Kendrix?" Just saying her name has my heart squeezing in my chest.

"Yes. I don't want to have this conversation with her over the phone. It needs to be in person. That gives me a few days to wrap my head around this. You know that your story, the version you told me, means that my mother lied to me. You know that, right? It means my mother denied my baby girl her father." Her voice cracks and I want nothing more than to wrap her in my arms and assure her that everything is going to be fine. *We're* going to be fine.

"Have dinner with me tonight?"

"I—" She pauses, her blue eyes boring into mine as if trying to decide. She's wavering. "Okay. I'll meet you somewhere. What I did last night, it was reckless and unsafe."

I flinch as if she slapped me across the face. "Unsafe?" The words feel like sandpaper in my mouth. "Did I scare you? God, Delaney, I would never hurt you. Never."

"No. No, it's not that. It's just that I don't know you."

"You know me. I'm the man who visits you in your dreams every night. I'm the man who holds you right here." I place my hand over my heart. "You're safe with me, but I don't want to push you. I never want you to feel uncomfortable or unsafe around me."

"That's the scary part," she whispers. "I didn't feel any of those things. I've never felt more... at home than I did sitting at your kitchen table." Her eyes well with tears, but they never fall. "I want to know you. I want all these memories that you keep telling me about. I-I know this makes me sound crazy, but I feel them. It's as if I know what you're telling me is true. My body knows you, but my mind... my mind only knows you in my dreams. Then there's my mother and what she's told me. I can't mold the two together. If you are Kendrix's father, you're not the man my mother warned me about. Was there someone else? Was I sleeping with two men?" She's getting agitated.

"Hey." I step close to her and place my hands on her shoulders. "It was just us, baby. I promise you that. That's not who you were. Deep in my soul, I know that's not what happened. Tell me what to do, Laney. How can I help you?"

"Give me time? I know that's a lot to ask, but this is a lot to take in. And—" She stops herself, biting down on her bottom lip.

"And what?"

Blue eyes wet with tears capture me. I couldn't look away from her if I tried. "I want you to be right. I can't explain it, but I-I want you to be right."

Not able to hold back, I pull her into my chest and hold her tight. Burying my face in her hair, I breathe her in and hope like hell her memories come back to her. Then I have to plead for her forgiveness, and well, if that never happens, it's my bed, and I'll have to lie in it. And if her memory never comes back, I send up a silent prayer that I can make her fall in love with me all over again.

Both of them.

"I'm right here, Laney. You take all the time you need. I'm not going anywhere. I'll do anything I can to help you remember."

She doesn't say anything, but that's okay because her body language tells me all I need to know. She relaxes into me, and her arms move around my waist as she returns my hug. She feels it—this connection we share—and I'll be damned if I'm going to let her forget it. I won't push her, though. I won't make demands.

Not yet.

I still have a chance, and I'm not going down without a fight.

Chapter 7

Delaney

I have a crush. Kenton Baldwin is unlike anyone I've ever met. And his tattoos... they're sexy as hell, and I find myself fantasizing about tracing them with my tongue. Beyond his sex appeal, he's attentive, kind, and he gives off this... protective aura. I barely know him, but I'm confident when I say that I'm safe with him. There is just something about him.

We had dinner last night. He allowed me the freedom of meeting him at the small mom and pop diner, but it's silly. I know he's a good man. I can feel it deep in my gut. What's stopping me is also in my gut, though. The butterflies. There is a colony of damn butterflies living in my belly, and they take flight when he's near. The sound of his voice, hell, even when I think about him, they flutter around like crazy.

I've never felt this kind of connection with anyone, let alone anyone I just met. That makes me believe his story even more. We meant something to each other. My thoughts stray to my mother. I've talked to her no less than twice a day since I've arrived and haven't said a word to her about what I've discovered. She hasn't mentioned anything other than her disagreement when I tell her how amazing this house is. I can't help but wonder if it really is the house and the people in this town or simply one person. Is it Kent? Is that why she's hell-bent on not living in Jackson? Is that why she tried to keep me from coming here? And she was adamant that Kendrix stayed with her. Claiming it was best to check the house out first. Was she afraid he would see her? Then why is she coming now? She's whining about coming, but she's not fighting me on it. I have so many unanswered questions.

"Morning, Delaney." The guy with the long hair waves as he walks through the door.

"Morning...." I let the greeting hang, realizing I don't know who is who. Kent has told me all about each of them, but my brain is in information overload.

"Seth." He grins.

"Morning, Seth." I nod, giving him a small grateful yet apologetic smile for not knowing him.

"Do I need to tell your wife you're flirting with my girl?" Kent's husky voice asks.

I pull my attention from Seth to see Kent standing in the doorway, a huge smile on his face. My palm automatically goes to my cheek and presses against where he kissed me goodbye last night on the sidewalk outside the diner and then again when I got home. The crazy man followed me all the way here and parked behind my rental, walking me to the door and giving me a second goodnight kiss on the same cheek. Who does that? He's gone out of his way to prove to me he's a man worthy of my affections. Last night, he apologized yet again for standing me up that night. I don't remember it, and he could easily have lied and told me all had been good with us, but he's not. His honesty is refreshing in light of all that I've learned on this trip. With each passing hour, I know my mother is lying. It's a gut feeling.

"Speaking of my wife, we're having dinner at our place. You're more than welcome to come." He points over his shoulder. "Have this one show you the way." With that, he winks and struts down the hallway.

Kent chuckles. "We're close, but I've told you that. The wives, they take turns having dinner at each other's houses. It's loud and chaotic, but I wouldn't change it for anything."

"Sounds like a good time."

"It is. What do you say? Will you come with me?"

"Kent, I don't know. I still need to talk to my mother, and—" I pause because I really don't have a good excuse.

"I want you there, Laney. So many times I've imagined what it would be like if I hadn't had my head shoved so far up my ass that night that you were a permanent part of my life. I imagine how life would be if I wouldn't have fucked up and lost you. Please say you'll come with me. I want you to meet them. Even more so, I want them to meet you."

How do I say no to that? Simple, I don't. Besides, I don't want to. I want to spend more time with him and meet the friends who he regards as family. "Okay."

Blinding. The smile he gives me is blinding, so much so, it makes his dark eyes sparkle. "Okay. Great. I'll um, I'll text you the address." He reaches for his phone, but my hand on his arm stops him.

"I'd like to ride with you. If that's all right?"

Before I know what's happening, he slides his hand behind my neck and pulls me close, resting his forehead against mine. "Do you know how bad I want to kiss you right now? It's been too fucking long since my lips have tasted yours." His words are a whispered yet throaty growl that causes those damn butterflies to take flight.

"Yo, Baldwin, let's go!" I hear one of the guys yell, followed by laughter. No doubt they've caught up, but I can't pry myself from Kent's gaze to check. Not that I care. We're adults and have nothing to hide.

"I need to go." Pulling back, he places his lips on my forehead. "Six o'clock, Laney. I'll be here at six o'clock."

I nod as my voice doesn't work. Not when the desire that pools between us is threatening to choke me. It's unlike anything I've ever felt or been a part of in my lifetime. Sure, I can't remember the majority of my adult life, but this… these moments with him. They're moments in time that I will always cherish. No matter if my memory comes back or not. No matter if his story matches up or not. I'll always have these moments, these feelings to look back on.

KAYLEE RYAN

A few hours later, I'm hanging out in the living room, just hoping to catch a glimpse of Kent. I feel like a damn sixteen-year-old. I'm shameless as I sit with my Kindle reading the same damn page over and over and over again. My eyes dart from my screen to the hallway. I'm ashamed to admit my Kindle has shut itself off a couple of times from my lack of page-turning activity.

My phone rings, and I smile when I see a video call from Mom. "Hello," I answer, holding the phone up to my face.

"Hi, Momma." My sweet daughter smiles into the phone. "Gram said we're going on a plane."

"That's right. Mommy is in Tennessee, and you and Gram are going to come and stay with me for a few days."

"Yay. I missed you so so much."

"I miss you too, baby." I'm smiling at her, watching her face light up with happiness. That's the only reason I missed him. It's not until his shadow stands over me that I look up to find Kent watching me.

His hands are fisted at his sides, and his jaw is clenched. He looks angry, and for the first time through all of this, I put myself in his shoes. If what he says is right, and he's her father. He's missed this. He's missed her smiles and her phone calls. The *love yous* and the *I miss yous*. He's never been witness to a nighttime hug from Kendrix, and let me tell you, her hugs are the best. I don't blame him for being angry. In fact, I think he's handled this so much better than I could have imagined.

"What's that noise?" Kendrix scrunches up her little nose, and I can't help it, I laugh at her cuteness.

"That's the construction crew. They're working on remodeling Great Gram and Gramps's house." I'm always honest with her and speak to her as if she's a little adult. I think it's because, as an adult, I often feel like a child. With missing parts of my life hanging in the balance, I feel lonely most days and out of control. Kendrix, she's been my saving grace through all of this, and I never want her to feel less than the incredible woman she can become.

"Oh, can I see?" she asks.

I glance up at Kent and he's still staring, but he's not staring at me. He's staring at the back of my phone. His eyes are transfixed from the sound of what could be his daughter's voice. I've only known him a few

60

days, from my current memories, and I want her to be his. I'm not sure what that says about me.

"Sure, sweetie." Without warning, I turn the phone so she can see the living room and part of the kitchen that's been demolished. I don't stop, letting the phone pass over Kent.

"Hi," Kendrix says in her chipper voice. "I'm Kendrix, I'm four. What's your name?" she asks.

My hand freezes as I watch him lay his eyes on her. "H-Hi." Kent waves to her. "I'm Kent."

"Hey, your name has Ken in it too. My mommy says my name is really special. She loved it so so much, but it made Grams sad."

Kent's eyes flash to mine before quickly darting back to the phone. I should pull it away, bring her attention back to me, but I can't seem to make my hand move. Maybe this is good. Get her used to seeing him. Kenton Baldwin is a force and I know that if these results come back that he is her father, he's going to steamroll into our lives. Funny, that doesn't sound bad to me.

"Your name is beautiful. Just like you. You look like your momma."

He's right. She does look just like me. She has my facial features, all except my nose. Her hair is that inky black that matches his to a T. "Thanks. What's that?" She points to his hand.

"Oh, this is a hammer." He holds it up so she can get a better look.

"What do you do with a hammer?" she asks him, and I know without seeing her that that little nose of hers, the one that matches her father's, is scrunched up.

His attention is on my phone. All for her, and it gives me some time to study him. To really take him in, and I see it. The same slope of the nose, and even her cheekbones. The ones I always thought resembled mine, they're his. I never had anyone to compare them to. But as I sit here and listen to him explain a hammer and nails and building supplies, I see it.

He's her father.

My breath hitches at what that means for me. Someone is lying. Is it my mother? Is it Kenton? He seems so genuine, and the way his eyes are glued to my phone, not willing to miss a single second I'm allowing him with my daughter, with *our* daughter, doubt creeps in. Either way,

I've been lied to. My mind whirls, and I hate to say this, but I believe him. My mother has always been a control freak. I've never known her to stoop to this level, but she thrives on having control. Kent, he seems to thrive on me, and now our daughter. I'm still going to go through with the test, but I know what the results will be.

After all this time, the missing piece of the puzzle has appeared. I can put a name and meaning behind the man I've been dreaming about. It also explains why I feel so comfortable and safe with him. He meant something to me.

My mother is the villain here. I feel it deep in my gut, the one that never steers me wrong. I feel a hand on my shoulder, and I jolt, looking up to find Kent's eyes on my phone, but the gentle brush of his thumb tells me he's aware of me and my lack of focus.

"Okay, sweetie." I turn the phone to face me, and Kent steps close. "You better give the phone back to Gram. I can't wait to see you tomorrow and I'm going to give you the biggest hug you've ever received."

"Yay, I like hugs, Momma. And, Mr. Kent, he said I could hammer a nail. Can I, Momma?"

My eyes find his, and he shrugs sheepishly. "Yeah, sweetie. You can learn how to hammer a nail from Mr. Kent. But," I add, "let's keep this a secret, okay? Don't tell Gram. That way, when you learn, you can surprise her."

"Oh, I'm good at that, aren't I, Momma? I'm good at surprises."

"Yes, sweetie, you are. Mommy loves you."

"Love you, bye, Momma." She waves, and the screen goes black.

As soon as my hand falls, I'm engulfed in a hug. Strong arms wrap around me, and this time, his hold is firm. "Laney." His voice cracks. "She's fucking incredible," he murmurs.

Did you hear that? That was my heart cracking wide open. Not just for him, but for Kendrix and for me. For the family we could have been. For the time we've all lost together. I'm angry. As my earlier revelations settle inside me, it takes everything I have not to call my mother and demand answers. But I want to watch her squirm. No way could this man be the one who tore us apart. I refuse to believe it.

When he finally pulls back, his eyes are misty, and I have to swallow back the lump in my throat. "Thank you. For letting me see her, for letting me talk to her. Just… thank you, Laney. God, she's incredible. So smart and curious. She's mine, Laney. I promise you that little girl is a part of me. There is no other explanation for the way I'm feeling right now."

"I know."

"What?" Shock is written all over his face.

"I don't know how or why, but I believe she's your daughter. That she's our daughter."

"Fuck." He crushes me to his chest once more, and this time, I squeeze him just as tight.

Chapter 8

KENT

My emotions are all over the place. One minute I'm pissed off because of the time I lost with them—moments of my daughter's life I'll never get back. Then, I'm sad. Not for me, as much for Delaney and Kendrix. They've been living a lie by thinking I didn't want them. I can't imagine what that must have felt like for her. Waking up, finding out you're pregnant, and thinking the father of your child doesn't want you. That's when the anger kicks back in, and it's all toward her parents. How could they do this to her? To both of them? I don't know how they sleep at night knowing that they kept that little girl from her father. And just thinking about her, about Kendrix and her bright smile, her curious mind, and the happiness takes over.

When I heard Delaney talking to her earlier, I was angry because I couldn't do the same. I feel it deep in my soul that little girl is a part of me. I can't explain it and I don't want to. I know the truth, and soon, we'll have the official documents to prove it. I just wanted to get a glimpse of her. To see the smile that shined through her voice, the smile of my little girl. I didn't expect Delaney to turn her phone toward me. I didn't expect her to let me actually talk to her. It's a moment I will never, for the rest of my life, ever forget. The day I met my daughter. The only thing that can top this is when I get to see her in person. When I get to tell her who I am and pull her into a hug. That moment is one I've not stopped thinking about since the moment I learned of her existence.

It's five minutes before six when I pull back into Delaney's driveway. I rushed home and took the world's fastest shower to get back to her. I'm still shocked she agreed to come with me tonight, but then again, earlier today, she rocked my world when she said she believed me that Kendrix is mine. I'm dying to ask her all day if she remembers me. If she remembers us. So many times I started to abandon the job and go in search of her, but I couldn't do that to the guys. We're a five-man crew for a reason, all hands on deck. Besides, I've been distracted enough on this job. I need to make sure I'm pulling my weight and not leaving them to pick up my slack.

Leaving the truck running, I climb out to greet her. She's already walking down the front steps of the porch by the time I reach her. Her long blonde hair is in curls hanging down her back, and her blue eyes are bright. She smiles at me, but I can tell she's nervous.

"Hey." I stop in front of her. I'm a step below so she's more my height. Not able to help myself, I lean in, wrapping my arms around her in a hug.

"Hi, Kenton," she whispers.

"You know you only used to call me Kenton when you were mad at me."

"Oh, yeah?" she asks, taking my offered hand and letting me lead her to the passenger side of my truck. I open the door for her and wait until she's strapped in before shutting the door and racing back to slide behind the wheel. "Did I get mad at you often?" she questions.

"Usually only during sex." Her quick intake of breath tells me I've shocked her.

"What?" She whips her head to the left to face me. "I'm going to need you to explain that one."

I chuckle. "I used to hold off on your pleasure. Push you to the point of no return and then back off." My voice is deep and husky, and my cock twitches thinking about making love to her. I've been inside her more times than I could possibly count, and my cock remembers. *I* remember. I keep my eyes trained on the road, but I can feel her stare.

66

"You did?" she breathes.

She doesn't remember. "I could never get enough of you. I liked to drag out your pleasure. I thrived on making you want me."

"H-How?" I glance over to see her swallow hard. "How did you make me want you?" Her voice is soft.

My hands grip the wheel and I'm two seconds from pulling over to the side of this fucking road and showing her. I know she's not ready for that. I shift in my seat, trying to make room for my growing erection in my jeans. "You really want to know?" My voice is thick with desire as sparks ignite between us in the cab of my truck.

Her reply is whispered, but it could have been yelling for the resounding sound in my ears. "Yes." No hesitation.

We're about two miles from Seth's place, but I have to pull over for this. Slowing down, I turn my truck into the driveway of a home on the market. I've driven past here enough times to know the house is vacant. I won't have to worry about getting run off. I pull up to the house, so we're away from the main road, put the truck in Park, and kill the headlights.

"Is this Seth's house?"

"No." I take off my seat belt and turn to face her.

"Where are we?" she asks. The lights from inside the cab of the truck are enough for me to see the concern on her face.

"You wanted to know. You wanted me to tell you how I would make you want me. I can't tell you that while I'm driving."

"Oh." Her mouth forms the cutest O, and I want nothing more than to kiss the shocked expression from her face.

"Laney." I reach over and cradle her cheek in the palm of my hand. "I promised myself I'd never lie to you. Never again. You sure you want to hear this?"

"I-Is it bad?"

"No, babe. It's not bad, but I'm not going to hold back. Never again will I hold back with you."

She nods. "Tell me, Kenton."

With my thumb, I trace her cheekbone, her blue eyes flare with heat, and there's a damn good chance that this conversation is going to kill me. "Your skin is so soft. I would spend hours tracing it with my tongue. I'd start with your lips, travel down your neck, and then…" I raise my hand that's not cradling her cheek and slip it inside her coat. Even with the layers of warmth, her nipples are hard. I run the pad of my thumb over the pebbled bud and she sucks in a breath at the contact. "So responsive," I murmur. "I could get you close, your orgasm at the cusp just by giving all of my attention to your breasts." I cup one in the palm of my hand, feeling its weight.

"I never let it get that far. Just when you were teetering on the edge, I'd pull away." My hand moves over her shirt and traces down her belly. "I'd continue my exploration, kissing, licking, nipping, and tasting you. I wouldn't stop until I reached your pussy." She shifts in her seat, but she's restricted by the seat belt. With deft fingers, I release her from confinement, and she angles her body toward mine. I'm cussing the console that's between us. There's something to be said about bench seats when you're trying to make a move on your girl.

"T-Then what?" Her voice is throaty and husky with desire. She rubs her thighs together to ward off the ache, one that I am more than willing to take care of for her. We're not there yet. I need those results in my hand. I need that printed proof that everything I'm telling her is true.

I open my mouth to tell her when her phone rings. She pulls away and I drop my hands. She fumbles with her purse and pulls her phone out. *Mom* flashes on the screen. "Hello," she answers, her voice sounding as if she just ran a marathon. Her wide eyes flash to mine, and I wink at her. "No, I'm fine. I had to run to my phone. I left it in the other room." She's quiet as she listens and I take the opportunity to think about anything other than devouring her, or describing in detail what I was about to do to her next in my mind.

Fluffy puppies.

Unicorns.

Grandma Baldwin.

"Hi, baby," she says, and instantly she has my attention. "I miss you too. I can't wait to see you tomorrow." She pauses, listening to our daughter, and I hate that I can't hear her sweet angelic voice. Delaney reaches over and laces her fingers through mine. I look down at our combined hands so I don't see what Delaney is doing, but when

Kendrix's sweet voice fills the cab of my truck, I know she's put her on speaker for me.

"I'm going to be high in the sky like the birds," my daughter states proudly.

"You are." Delaney laughs. "You be sure to stay close to Gram and listen to what she tells you."

"I will, Mommy. I love you."

"I love you too, sweetie. Goodnight."

"Night." The truck goes silent and the call is ended. "She's excited," Delaney speaks up.

"I can tell. Her first time flying?"

"Yeah. We've never left California. It was my first time too, since the accident."

"How did you do?"

"Great. Mom had my anxiety at an all-time high. Telling me how much she hated Jackson and that the people were rude. She couldn't have been more off base."

"She wanted to keep you, both of you from me."

"I'm so sorry," she whispers.

"No. This isn't your fault. You have nothing to be sorry for. You said earlier today that you believe me, that Kendrix is mine. Do you remember?"

"No. But she looks like you."

"That's it? That's what you're going off?"

"That and the fact that my gut tells me what you're saying is true. What would be your motivation? Since the moment you laid eyes on me, you've been dedicated to me believing that we meant something to each other. You've been patient with me, and the sparkle in your eyes when you gaze at me... it's a look I've never seen before. At least not directed at me. And when you talked to her today, your eyes lit up. Why would you be happy to talk to my daughter if she wasn't yours as well? You believe it, and in my gut, I feel as though I can trust you. That the words you say are true."

"And your mother?"

"I'm waiting to talk to her face-to-face. I want to watch her reaction when I talk to her. When I ask her about you, about why she lied to me."

"Do you want me there with you?"

She reaches over and rests her hand on my arm. "No, but thank you for offering."

"When do I get to see her? Kendrix?"

"Well, the test is Friday at the house, right?"

"Yeah."

"You'll be working all day I suspect."

"I will be, yes."

"And you told our daughter that you would teach her how to hammer a nail?"

I can't hide my grin when she says "our daughter" or the excitement I feel at her words. "Are you going to let me do that?"

"We can't tell her who you really are until we get the results. Not because I don't believe you. I do, and I want to. I want you to be her father. I just… I think I need to have that paper in my hand, you know? I need to have concrete proof because my mind isn't there. All these years I've had no other choice but to believe what others have told me. I had no reason to believe they were telling me lies, and now this. Now I find you. I just want the proof. I need it."

I understand where she's coming from. I hate it, but I understand it. "Okay."

"Just like that? No argument?"

"No. I want to spend time with her. I want to get to know my daughter. Besides, it's just a few days, a week tops until we can tell her who I am. I can tell you this. I've lost almost five years with her. I won't lose another day. I will be in her life. I don't know what that means for the three of us, but I know what it means for me and Kendrix. I'll be where she is." There is conviction in my voice.

"I'd like that" is her reply, and I admit it's not the one I was expecting.

"We have dinner to get to. We're already late." Facing forward, I put on my seat belt and glance over to make sure that she's buckled in as well before driving the rest of the way to Seth's place. I park behind Ridge and turn off the truck. "Ready?" I ask her.

"What if they don't like me?"

"Impossible. They know what you mean to me."

"You told them?"

"No. Ridge knows. The guys all know we had something in the past. But, Laney, I never bring anyone with me. You being here, that tells them all that they need to know. You're important to me."

"Do they know about Kendrix?"

"Ridge does. The others, I haven't told them yet. And," I say, not giving her time to think negatively, "before you analyze why, I just needed to wrap my head around it all. And my friends, well, they rally. Not in a bad way, but once they find out, they're going to pull you into the fold, and you become one of us."

"That doesn't sound so bad."

"Yeah? Well, all right then. Looks like I got an announcement to make. Family dinner tonight has a reason after all."

"You don't have to tell them tonight. I mean, we can wait for the results."

"Why? I know it and you know it. I can't wait for the other kids to meet her." With that, I open the door and climb out of the truck. She meets me in front, and I lace my fingers with hers. "This okay?"

"Yeah, this is okay."

Hand in hand, we walk to the front door. I don't bother knocking— none of us ever do. We're family, and we all have an open-door policy. "Hello!" I call. I hear Knox yell, "Uncle Kent," and lots of little feet as they come barreling down the hall.

Chapter 9

Delaney

Little people are everywhere. As soon as Kent calls out our arrival, they swarm to us, smiling and laughing and vying for their uncle Kent's attention. He releases my hand and drops to his knees, passing out hugs and hellos. My heart swells and cracks at the same time—something I never knew was possible. My little girl missed out on this. She missed the love of this man, his hugs, and his smiles. His love.

"Who's that?" One of the adorable little boys points at me. He looks to be close to Kendrix's age.

"This is my friend Delaney."

"Hi." The little guy waves up at me. "You're really pretty."

I blush. That's what my life has come to. I blush when a child pays me a compliment. "Thank you." I crouch down to get to his level. "What's your name?"

"Knox Alexander Beckett. That's my sister. Her names Everly."

"It's nice to meet you, Knox." I hold out my hand and, like the little man he presents himself to be, he doesn't hesitate to put his in mine and shake.

"That's Everly." Kent points to two girls, who appear to be not much younger than Knox. "The one on the right is Everly, and Finley is on the left. These little monsters," he says, tickling the two little boys who look just alike and are sitting in his lap, "are Ben and Beck."

"And this little angel?" I ask, waving to a little girl who looks not much more than a year old.

"This is Daisy."

"Hi, Daisy." I hold my hand out to her, and hesitantly, she steps toward me. She looks over at Kent and he smiles at her and she changes course and tumbles into him and the twins.

"Come here, you." He grabs her and blows on her belly, making her laugh. The boys rush off and Daisy cuddles up in Kent's lap, content to stay where she is.

"They're all adorable."

"We have one more. Ryder is three months, so he can't toddle after me like the others, and then Tyler and Reagan are expecting number three—they have the twins—in a few months." I nod, taking it all in, and trying to memorize that the twins are Tyler and Reagan's. "She'll have lots of cousins. Lots of family to support her." Kent's voice is soft, almost reverent when he speaks of Kendrix.

"I'm not going to remember all of this."

He grins. "You'll catch on in no time. Come on. I want you to meet the wives and the guys officially, of course."

"Officially? Have I not already met them?"

"Yeah, but that was as Delaney, a girl from my past. The one that got away."

"As opposed to?"

He smirks and shrugs, lacing his fingers through mine and pulling me further into the house.

"There he is." Tyler smiles as we enter the kitchen.

"Hey." Kent waves to the group. "Everyone, I'd like for you to meet Delaney."

Before I know what's happening, the women in the room rush to me, all of them taking turns giving me a hug and welcoming me. "I'm Mara," the last one says. "I know you're not going to remember all of us, but that one's mine." She points to Seth. "Welcome. What would you like to drink?" she asks.

"Uh, just water is fine. Thank you." She nods, and before she can turn to retrieve a water, Seth is there handing it to her, making her laugh. "Thank you," I tell them both.

"All right, boys, now that all the ladies are here, we're going to chat. Pizza will be here in fifteen." Mara grins. She takes hold of my hand and pulls me behind her to the living room. "I cheated," she says when we're all seated.

"Pfft," another one speaks up. "It's food, and the kids will love it. No one ever said family dinners had to be homemade."

"Exactly," another woman agrees before turning to me. "Ridge is mine." She smiles. "Kendall." She goes on to tell me her kids, and then each of the women takes a turn doing the same.

"I'm sorry if I don't remember all of this," I tell them.

Mara waves her hand in the air. "You'll get it. There's a lot of us, and as the newest member of this brood, I can tell you it can be a lot to take in." She gives me a kind smile that has me relaxing even further into the couch.

"Your home is beautiful," one of them says. I think her name was Reagan.

"Thank you."

"When we were kids, we would always call it the castle." She laughs. "I can't imagine living there."

"I can't either," I confess. They give me an odd look, and I realize Kent really hasn't told them much about me. About us. "I was in a car accident a few years ago. I lost my memory." Their reactions range from gasping to hands covering their mouths, and whispers of sympathy. "When I woke up, I didn't know anyone. But within a couple of months, I had most of my memory back, as far as we can tell, except for anything beyond my high school graduation, which is when we moved here." I see the confusion in their eyes and I'm sure they're only holding back because we just met. "I don't remember Kenton," I say softly. "He remembers me. He has a picture of us on his phone. We looked happy."

"I can't imagine how that must be for you." Mara reaches over and gently squeezes my arm, giving me a kind smile.

"I have a daughter," I tell them. "She's going to be five in March." I don't look or make eye contact with any of them while I pull my phone out of my back pocket and scroll to a picture of Kendrix. I hand it to Mara.

"Oh my God," she says breathily.

"Can we see?" another asks. I think her name is Dawn.

I nod, and they each pass the phone around. All of them have the same reaction. When I finally have my phone back in my hands, I take another look at my baby girl. I miss her so much. I can't wait to wrap my arms around her tomorrow. Locking the screen, I place my phone back in my pocket and look up at them. Four sets of eyes are watching me closely. "Say it." I smile, fighting back my anxiety.

"She looks just like him," all four of them say at the same time.

Emotion builds inside me. I don't want to break down in front of these women who I just met, but everything comes crashing in around me, and I can't seem to stop it. I suck in a breath, trying to ward off the tears, but I lose the battle as they slide over my cheeks.

"We're going down in the basement!" Mara yells into the kitchen. She stands and offers me her hand. I take it, standing as well. The other three are suddenly there, surrounding me. Together, the five of us make our way downstairs. "They won't let the kids down here," Mara explains. "They also won't come down here. Not for a while. They'll assume we're in the craft room." She points to a door down the hall. "Sit." She guides our group to the huge sectional couch.

"Reagan, Ridge's sister," one of the women speaks and waves with a smile. "I know you don't know us, Delaney, but I promise you we're on your team. You can tell us anything and we'll keep that shit locked tight." She grins.

"Kendall." Another smiles. "Ridge's wife." Without me having to tell them, they know it's a lot for me to take on. Maybe it's because they now know I lost my memory and they think I need it. Regardless, I appreciate it. And I think I've got them all down, at least for tonight. "You can talk to us. In fact, what's your number?" She pulls her cell out, and I rattle off my digits. "I'll text it to everyone, and we'll send you ours. If you need us for anything, don't hesitate." The others in the group murmur their agreement and my heart swells.

"I'm glad he has you. Kenton," I clarify. "I don't remember my time with him, but I'm glad he has this support system."

"What about you?"

I blow out a breath. "Well, my mother told me when I woke up, before I could remember anyone or anything, that the father of my child told me to take care of it. That he didn't want me. She assured me he wasn't worth my time or memories. She had me convinced that the reason I didn't remember those few years is because of him. That he wasn't a good guy and that my daughter and I were better off without him."

"Holy shit," Dawn says, and quickly smacks her hand over her mouth, making me laugh.

"Right? So, I come here after she begs me not to. My dad left the Nottingham Estate to me in his will. He passed about a year ago." They speak their condolences, and I move on. I tell them the entire story about Mom not wanting me to come here. How she had me thinking that Tennessee was the state of the mean people—or the devil is more like what she wanted me to believe. I lay it all out on the table for them.

"Wow," Kendall says, sitting back against the couch and crossing her arms over her chest. "I don't know that I have words for that. She couldn't have been talking about Kent. He's one of the nicest guys you'll ever meet."

"Yeah, he seems to be." I go on to tell them about the day he first saw me and his reaction to me not knowing him, and then every detail since. "I didn't realize I needed this, to talk about this until tonight," I tell them. "Thank you for listening."

"Of course." This from Mara.

"What's her name? Your daughter?" Reagan asks.

I don't even try to hide my smile. "Kendrix." I wait, letting it sink in. "My mother hated it. Still hates it to this day. She didn't speak to me for days after she was born."

"She knew." Kendall points her finger at me. "That's dirty."

I nod. "It's hard for me, but just in a few days of being with Kent, talking to him, I believe him. I see him in my dreams. I have for years. It's always the same thing, he's reaching out for me to come with him. I wake up before I can take his hand. The same dream over and over and over again."

"Aw," Dawn says. She presses her hands to her chest. "It's like a real-life fairy tale."

"I haven't talked to my mother about all of this yet. She and Kendrix fly in tomorrow. I wanted to ask her face-to-face. I need to see her reaction when I ask her all of this."

"What can we do?" Kendall asks.

My heart swells. I'm so happy Kent has these amazing women surrounding him. Supporting him. And if what my heart feels is right, my daughter too. I don't know what that means for me, but right now, they're in my corner as well, and it brings tears to my eyes. "Nothing. You've done so much by listening. This is all such a huge mess."

"What about Kendrix? She's coming with your mother, right?" Kendall asks.

"She is. I can't wait to see her. It's only been five days, but I miss her so much."

"How about a play date?" Kendall offers.

"Definitely," Mara chimes in. "Finley would love that."

"The boys too." Reagan nods.

"Daisy loves her cousins," Dawn adds.

"This way, she doesn't have to be there in case things get heated. I assume you don't want her with Kent, at least not just the two of them. Not until she knows him."

"We're getting a paternity test. Just for the concrete proof since I can't remember," I say sadly.

"Right. And even though your heart tells you what he's saying is true, even though you can see him in her when you look at them, you're a momma. We have to keep our babies safe, even from heartbreak." Mara smiles kindly.

"I know you don't know us," Reagan tells me. "But we're good people. You can trust us with her."

"I can feel that. I know that sounds crazy, but you've all been so welcoming. I can't thank you enough for that."

"Okay, so how about you bring her here tomorrow? Or I can come and pick her up?" Mara offers.

"Thank you. Let me think about it. Maybe see how things go. My mother is not the yelling type. She's more the silent treatment, but I can't promise that I won't lose my cool. That's not me, but she lied to me. She denied my little girl her daddy. I don't remember him, but in the short time I've spent with him this week, I know without a doubt he would have been there."

"He wouldn't have missed a single second of it." Reagan smiles, wiping at her eyes.

"Well, you have our numbers, or you will," Dawn says, pulling her phone out of her pocket. Her fingers fly across the screen, and I feel my back pocket vibrate. This happens three more times as all of them send me a message.

"I appreciate you all. Thank you. I hope I don't need it, but I would like to get the kids together. Let them play. That way, if the need does arise, Kendrix will feel more comfortable. However, my little girl doesn't really know a stranger. It doesn't surprise me that she's taken so well to him and his friends."

"She's going to fit right in with this brood."

"Babe," a deep male voice calls down the steps. "Pizza's here."

"Let's go eat."

Upstairs, the kids are all sitting at two small kids' tables. Kendrix has the same Little Tykes table in her room. That's where we have our tea parties. They're munching away on pizza, which is cut up into small pieces, with sippy cups in front of them. There is a napkin tucked under each plate that none of them are using, which makes me smile. The daddies dote on their kids. They're involved, and it makes me miss my own father. He was hands-on every step of the way. I am the epitome of a daddy's little girl.

The adults are gathered around the huge dining room table. We each take our seats and Kent immediately leans in close.

"You doing okay?"

"Yes." I smile at him. His concern touches me. With every interaction, he cements my gut feeling that he's a good guy. The kind who tells the truth. I wish I could say that my mother falls into that category, but unfortunately, that's not possible. I'm dreading this confrontation with her, but I push that out of my mind and just enjoy the night.

"Well, since everyone's here, we have something to say," Mark says and looks at Dawn and smiles. The one look says so much. You can see it in his eyes that she's his entire world. "We're having a baby." He never takes his eyes off his wife.

Cheers, murmurs of congratulations, and hugs are passed around. "It's really early." Dawn smiles. "We were going to keep it to just us until we were past the first trimester, but this guy"—she points to Mark, who has his arm around her where they sit side by side at the table—"he couldn't hold it in any longer."

"I'm so excited. Our babies will be close together," Reagan says.

"Baby," Tyler chimes in, "*one* baby," making us all laugh.

"Right. It's been confirmed. Only one this time." Reagan grins up at her husband.

A pang of jealousy hits me. I missed this. All of it. I didn't get to celebrate and share that connection. Life isn't fair, and I understand that, but I still wish things could have been different. I wish that I would have had moments like these.

"Next time," Kent whispers in my ear. I turn to look at him, raising my eyebrows in question. "I hate that we missed all this, Laney. But we can't change the past, but the future, that's ours." He kisses my cheek and turns back to the table.

My heart races as I look around to see if anyone heard him, but then I realize that even if they did, it doesn't matter. We're adults. Our life is our own, and it's what we make of it. That's not something I've practiced in my adult life, at least not the parts I can remember. I've always let my mother lead, and the more time I spend with this amazing man at my side, and his friends, I realize the error of my ways. I was so lost, depressed, and I let her run my life. That stops now.

The future is ours.

Chapter 10

KENT

I didn't sleep. I tossed and turned all night long. Today's the day I get to meet my daughter. I get to set my eyes on her in the flesh, and I'm nervous as hell. What if she doesn't like me? She's not going to know I'm her father, not until we get the results back, and I get it. I understand the need that Delaney has to have concrete proof since she doesn't have her memories. I get it. I fucking hate it, but I get it. So I have to wait, and I hate waiting.

Throwing the covers off, I climb out of bed and head to the shower. As the hot water rains down on me, I think about Delaney and Kendrix. About what it would be like to wake up with Delaney in my arms and to get hugs from my daughter when she's sleepy and wants to cuddle. Having breakfast together, bedtime stories… all of it. I can't shut it off. I can't stop thinking about all the time we missed, and all the time I have to make up for.

Wiping the steam from the mirror, I take a long hard look at the man staring back at me. I've never been ashamed of my ink, or the life I've chosen to live, but what if my choices are the reason they decide I'm not what they want? I know I get judged for my ink. While the guys all have tattoos as well, I took mine to an all-new level. It became somewhat of an addiction after I lost Delaney. I don't know why, but it did and it's where we are. I've never regretted any of them, but what if she's afraid of me? What if my daughter is scared of me, from the choices I've made in my life? I can't handle that. Talking to her on the phone she seemed fine. However, face-to-face, up close and personal, I know I can be intimidating. I never want to be that to her. Not my little girl.

Bowing my head, I blow out a breath and reach for my toothbrush. I don't look in the mirror again. I can't. The worry is enough to choke me, and I feel as though I could suffocate in this bathroom. Once finished, I toss my toothbrush back into the holder, rinse out my mouth, wipe it with a towel, and shut off the light. I'm nervous enough I don't need to let my doubts and worries cloud my mind. I need to be clear-headed when I meet her.

Fuck.

I'm meeting my daughter.

Twenty minutes later, I'm pulling into the shop. Mara smiles wide, and so does Seth. "She told you," I say, shaking my head.

"Yes!" Mara squeals. "You get to see her today, right? Kendrix? She's coming today?" she says, practically bouncing with excitement.

"Yeah, they'll be here this afternoon." My eyes flash to Seth. "She fill you in?"

He nods. "You should have told us."

"I know. It was a lot to wrap my head around. I wasn't keeping it from you."

"Look, Kent, I get it. Putting yourself out there, that shit's scary."

"Not anymore," I interrupt him. "I'm not scared of telling you how I feel about her. I'm nervous as hell to meet my daughter." Before I can go on, Ridge, Mark, and Tyler walk in, and I can tell that their wives have all filled them in as well. "Like I said, I'm not scared to admit what she means to me, what she's always meant to me. I'm nervous as hell to be meeting my daughter."

"You sure she's yours?" Tyler asks.

I don't answer him. Instead, I pull out my phone and scroll to the picture of Kendrix. I hand him my phone. I'm not offended at his question. This is all coming out of left field for them, and that's on me. I never should have kept her a secret. I should have screamed from the rooftops that she was mine. Then, maybe, just maybe, she never would have been in the accident. I would have been with her that night. She could have told me about the baby, and I would have kept her with me.

Always.

I never would have missed her growing round with our child. I would have been there the moment my baby took her first breath. I would have been there for every moment. Instead, I ran scared. Went to Bottom's Up with the guys, had a few beers, wallowed in the fact that she meant something to me. I should have been a man. Instead, I acted like a coward. So, while Delaney's mother is to blame, so I am. That's something that I'll have to live with for the rest of my life.

"She's a cute kid. Looks just like you. But those eyes, those are all her momma," Mark says, handing me my phone.

"She's the perfect mix of both of us."

They nod. Just like that, I have their acceptance and support. "We're having a test done. I don't need it. But Laney, she doesn't remember us. I mean, she dreams about me." I go on to explain the dreams, and they don't look surprised, so I'm guessing Delaney told the girls all about it, which in turn, they filled their husbands in.

"Good to have it in writing," Seth says.

"Yeah."

"How you holding up?" Mara asks.

"I'm a nervous fucking wreck, but I don't think I've ever been more excited about anything in my entire life."

Her eyes soften. She stands from her desk and comes around to wrap me in a hug. "We're all here for you. We told Delaney the same thing," she says, pulling back. Seth snakes his arm around her waist and pulls her into him. "She has our numbers. We offered to watch Kendrix in case things get heated, but she doesn't think that it's necessary. Apparently, her mom isn't much of a yeller. Delaney says she's more of the 'I'm going to ignore you and the situation' type."

"Yeah, I don't know about all that, but I appreciate you reaching out to her. I can't imagine what she's feeling, what's going through her head. I'm trying to not push her, but fuck, everything about her is familiar to me. It's ingrained in my memory. Every second, every minute I ever spent with her."

"They're your family, Kenton. That means that they're our family." Mara says it like it's the simplest of things.

She's right. It is that simple. We can't change the past. I need to stop dwelling on that and focus on what's important. Meeting my daughter. Making sure she knows how much I love her. I do. I've never met her, but I feel it in my heart. The minute I saw her on screen, I knew she was mine. And her momma, well, if I have my way, she's going to be mine too. She's always been mine. I just never told her. That's all about to change.

Delaney left over two hours ago to go to the airport. I'm trying not to worry, but it's hard not to. I've been shit help today, but the guys haven't said a word. My friends, my brothers from other mothers, have my back. The airport is about forty minutes away, so we're looking at an hour and twenty for drive time. Forty minutes is a stretch. They have to get their bags, and the plane could have been late, traffic…. I list off all the reasons they're not here yet.

"Wow. Momma, this house is so big. It's like Barbie's house," a sweet voice breaks into my thoughts.

I freeze.

"It's a big house, for sure."

"Like Barbie's," the sweet voice says again.

A smile spreads across my face, and I feel a hand clamp down on my shoulder. I turn to look and see Ridge. "You good?"

I nod. I can't speak.

"Are we going to live here?"

"No," a voice I recognize as Tillie Nottingham answers.

I ball my fists at my sides. "Mother," Delaney scolds her. "I'm not sure, sweetie," Delaney answers our daughter. "We'll just have to see how things turn out. You think you'd like living here?"

"Oh, yes," she says quickly. "It's pretty here, and it's not noisy outside like it is at home."

My smile is back.

"Hey, little lady," Seth says.

"Hi, are you Mr. Kent?" she asks with hope in her voice.

I swallow hard.

"No. My name is Seth. It's nice to meet you," he says. I can imagine he's holding his hand out for her.

I should be mad he's meeting her before me, but I can't be. She asked for me. My little girl asked for me. Yeah, I know she doesn't know who I am to her, but that one simple question, it restored all of my fear, spinning it into hope. With five words from my daughter, I know that everything is going to be okay.

"Do you hammer nails too? Mr. Kent said he would teach me," Kendrix says. "Oh, and my name is Kendrix Layne Nottingham."

"He did? Well, can I tell you a secret?"

"Oh, I'm good at secrets. Right, Momma?"

"You are, baby," Delaney agrees with her.

"Well, Mr. Kent, he's the best at hammering nails. I can do it, but he's so much better than me."

There's a shuffle of feet before she says, "Oh, is he here? I really want to hammer a nail."

Seth chuckles. "He's here. It was nice to meet you, Kendrix Layne Nottingham."

"Bye, Mr. Seth," she calls out, and I hear his heavy footfalls.

He appears in the door, and the smile on his face has jealousy pinching my gut. "She's all you, my man. No denying that. She's smart as a whip too. Wouldn't put it past her to figure it out on her own." He laughs, and something that feels like a flock of birds take flight in my gut.

"Momma, let's go find him. Please, Momma."

"No," Delaney's mom says again.

"Mother." Delaney's voice is stern. "I have you set up in the bedroom at the end of the hall on the second floor. Why don't you go lie down? Kendrix and I are going to find Kent."

"Delaney." Mrs. Nottingham's voice cracks.

"I know, Mother. I know it all. We'll discuss this later." She leaves no room for negotiation in her tone.

"I was protecting you. Both of you."

"From what? What were you protecting me from? Love? Strong work, Mother, you succeeded," Delaney spits out.

"He's—" her mom starts, only to be shut down again.

"Enough. You will say nothing further, do you understand me? You're in my house, Mother. And this is my life. You no longer get to run the show. I can't even look at you right now."

"Momma, what's wrong?" Kendrix asks, and I step toward the door. A hand on my shoulder stops me. I know it's Ridge without looking. He's been standing there since they got here.

"Nothing, sweetie. How about you and I go find Mr. Kent?"

"Yay. Momma, do you know how to hammer a nail?" she asks.

"I do, but I'm sure Mr. Kent is so much better than Mommy."

"Maybe he can teach you too?" Her sweet little voice is hopeful.

"I'm sure he will, sweetie."

Their footsteps grow closer. My eyes are glued to the door as I stand frozen, waiting to see her for the first time. When they step into the open doorway, my heart stalls in my chest.

My daughter.

My baby girl.

My world.

Delaney drops to her knees. I don't take my eyes off her as she brushes Kendrix's hair out of her face. "Mr. Kent, he's… a very special man to Mommy and to you."

"'Cause he's good at hammering nails?"

I hear the guys chuckle behind me, and my smile appears yet again. "I don't know about that. I'll let you be the judge. Kendrix, I'd like you to meet Kent." She points at me and I pull in a ragged breath.

Kendrix takes one step, and then another, and another until she's standing in front of me. I drop to my knees and just stare at her. She's beautiful. The perfect mix of Delaney and myself. I want nothing more than to hug her tight. Wrap my arms around her and never let her go.

"Hi." She waves. Her smile falters when she looks down at me.

"What's wrong, baby girl?"

"Where's your hammer?"

I chuckle. "You ready for me to teach you how to hammer a nail?"

She nods her little head up and down like a bobblehead on the dash of a car.

"Well, I have something for you."

I stand and walk over to the corner of the room. I grab the small kit I bought at Lowe's earlier this week when we were picking up supplies. It's for kids, with a small hammer and nails. It's in a pink gift bag, and I feel stupid for handing my little girl a gift she doesn't know is from her daddy. I crouch back to my knees to be on her level. I don't want to miss a minute of this moment.

"Oh, thank you. Can I open it, Momma?" She looks over her shoulder at Delaney, who nods.

My eyes find hers, which are misting with tears. Kendrix rips into the package, and the smile that lights up her face will remain with me until the day I take my last breath.

"Oh, it's all mine? I have my own hammer? Cool." She drops the bag and throws her arms around my neck. "Thank you, thank you, thank you," she says, her little voice right next to my ear.

I try to fight it. But I can't. I put my arms around her and hug her back. Emotion clogs my throat, and I blink rapidly, fighting back the tears. I don't want her to think I'm sad, especially when I'm the complete opposite. I'm happy. So fucking happy to finally be holding her in my arms.

"Can we do it now?" she asks.

"Sweetie." Delaney clears her throat. "Mr. Kent is working. I'm sure we can do it later."

"Hi." Ridge bends down and holds his hand out to her. "I'm Ridge."

"Hi, Mr. Ridge."

"You know, I think now is the perfect time for you and Mr. Kent to work on learning to hammer nails."

"Really?" she asks excitedly. She jumps and claps her hands. Then turns to face Delaney. "Did you hear, Momma? We can do it now." She whips back around, grabs the gift bag, and holds her hand out for me. "Ready, Mr. Kent?"

My daughter. "I'm ready." I look up at Delaney and she nods. "Let's go to the kitchen so you can sit at the table and be able to see what you're doing."

"But you hafta teach me," she says, putting me in my place.

"I will. I promise." In my head, I'm making her a million more promises. To always be there, to scare off her dates, to kiss her skinned knees, help with science fair projects, never miss a sporting event or any other major event in her life, and most of all, to never break her heart… just to name a few.

We make our way to the kitchen, and I open the package, setting it all out on the table. I take my time explaining the hammer and the safety of not smashing your fingers and being careful with the nails. Kendrix hangs on my every word. By the time we're finished, she's successfully built a small birdhouse.

"That was so much fun. I want to build more stuffs."

I laugh. "We can do that. I'll get some more. I think you're ready for some of your own tools too."

"Oh, I am," she agrees, nodding.

"We're wrapping up for the day," Mark says, sticking his head in the kitchen door.

"All right." I turn my attention back to my daughter. "I guess it's time for me to go home for the day."

"Aw, can you stay?"

Oh, baby girl. I wish I could. "Not today. But I'll be here tomorrow. I actually have an appointment. My doctor is coming here to test my spit," I say, wrinkling my nose.

"Ew, what's wrong with your spit?" she asks with a look of disgust on her face.

"Nothing. Just testing it out. Hey, you want to do it with me?"

"I don't know. What do I hafta do?"

"You know what a Q-tip is?"

She shakes her head. "When your momma cleans out your ears."

"Oh, those tickle." She laughs.

"Well, I have to open wide, and they swipe it across my cheek and that's it." I look up at Delaney and she nods. We didn't discuss how we were going to go about telling Kendrix about the test. It just kind of came to me and I blurted it out. And I want her to know that she's going to see me again tomorrow. And the next day and the next day. Every day for the rest of her life.

"Oh, do they do it back here?" She opens her mouth and points at her throat. "I don't like that," she tells me. "I was sick, and Momma had to hold my hand and the doctors choked me."

"They had to swab your throat to test for strep throat. They were not choking you," Delaney speaks up.

"I didn't like it, Momma."

"I know, sweetie, but it helped the doctors know how to treat you and make you feel all better."

Just something else I missed out on. I soak up every tidbit of information I can like a sponge. "That's it. Just the cheek." I open my mouth and show her.

"Okay. I can do that. Are you scared, Mr. Kent?"

"No, sweet girl. I'm not scared."

"Me either." She sits up straighter, squaring her little shoulders.

"Hey, Kendrix." I look up to see Ridge in the doorway. "Did you know that I have a son and a daughter close to your age?"

"You do?" Her little eyes grow wide.

"I do. In fact, they have lots of cousins too. How would you like to come over and play sometime?"

"Oh, Momma, can I? Please, can I?" She looks at Delaney and then turns back to Ridge. "Can I come today?"

He chuckles. "You're always welcome."

"Please, Momma. Oh, please."

"Sweetie, you don't know them."

"But Mr. Kent does. And Mr.…. I forget his name." She points at Ridge, making us all laugh.

"You sure you want to go?"

"I do. Mr. Kent, can we build more things?"

"Actually, we're making cookies at my house tonight," Ridge tells her.

"Oh!" she exclaims. "I love to make cookies. Please, Momma. Please, please, please."

"Okay," Delaney relents.

"Yay!" She climbs off the chair, and I reach out to hold it, so she doesn't topple over.

"Where are you going?" I ask her.

"To get my shoes. I'm making cookies with him." She points to Ridge and then races out of the room.

"We need to talk to her about stranger danger," I tell Delaney. I'm smiling but serious at the same time.

"I have. She doesn't see anyone as a stranger. They're all her friends."

"Kent used to be the same way. He was always the most outgoing out of all of us growing up," Ridge tells her.

"Really? I'm thinking we need to have a little chat. I need some dirt on this one."

"Nope. Closed book. You see, the five of us were inseparable, so if I give you his dirt, I'm also giving you mine." Ridge smirks.

"Ready," Kendrix announces. She has her coat on upside down and her shoes in her hands.

"All right, missy. How about I drive you over to Ridge's house, and you can make some cookies for a little while?"

"Yay. Let's go, Momma." She runs out of the room.

"Wait for me!" Delaney calls out to her. "Thank you, Ridge. Are you sure?"

"Positive. I know the wives offered, and you're worried, but I promise you, she's family. I'd never let anything happen to her."

I stand and go to Delaney, standing as close as I can without holding her. I don't want Kendrix to see that. Not yet. Not until I tell her that I'm her daddy. That day can't come soon enough. "Laney, do you want me here with you when you talk to your mother? Or I can to go to Ridge's with Kendrix."

She bites down on her bottom lip. "Can you go with her? I mean, I know we can trust them, you trust them, but I don't know them. I don't know you either, but I trust you. And I've seen you for years in my dreams, and she looks like you, and you have a picture of us, and all these stories, and..."

I lean in and kiss her cheek. "I understand, baby. She's safe with me. I promise you that, Laney. I hate that you can't remember our time together, but I promise you she's safe."

"I know."

Simple, complete acceptance. I know she feels this connection between us. I see it in her eyes. I just wish she could remember. I need to help her remember. I want her to have the same memories of our time together. Hell, I even want her to be mad at me for standing her up that night. I want it all. I'd rather fight with her and grovel at her feet than her not have those memories.

The memories of how it all began. The memories of conceiving our daughter.

"Let me get my coat." She walks out of the room.

"Thank you, man. I can't...." I run my hands through my hair.

"No worries, brother." Ridge nods and disappears.

I follow him to find Kendrix on the floor wrestling to get her shoes on. "You need some help?"

"Yes, please." She huffs and sits back, holding her weight on her arms. "This is hard work."

I don't hide my smile. "Good thing I was here to help."

"I'm a big girl," she tells me.

"You are. But sometimes it's okay even for big girls to ask for help."

"That's what my momma says to me."

"Your momma is a very smart woman."

"I's going to be like her when I get big."

"There you go." I finish with her second shoe. "Now, what do you say we do something about this coat?"

"It feels funny."

I make a silly face and she giggles, the sound cementing into my heart. "Well, it feels funny because you put it on upside down, you silly goose." I reach out and tap her nose with my index finger, and she cackles with laughter. The sound warms my soul. I help her out of her jacket and put it back on the correct way as Delaney joins us.

"Ready to go?"

"Where are you going?"

Tillie.

Delaney turns slowly to face her mother. "Where I'm going is none of your concern." Her voice is low and leaves zero room for negotiation.

"Are you taking her?"

"I am. I'll be back." She glances over at me.

"Thirty minutes," I say, reading her thoughts. She needed to know how far it was to Ridge's place and back.

"Thirty minutes," she tells her mother.

"Is she going with you?"

"Gram, I'm going to bake cookies," Kendrix says happily. She's blissfully unaware of what's going on, of the tension in the room between the adults.

"No."

"Excuse me, but she's my daughter. You have no say so in where she goes or who she's with."

"Delaney, I refuse—" she starts, but I stand up and she stops whatever bullshit she was going to spew.

"I'll be back in thirty minutes."

"Hand me your keys," I tell Delaney. "I'll go start your car."

She looks over at me, and her eyes soften. Reaching into her coat, she pulls out her keys and hands them over. "Thanks, Kent."

I give her shoulder a gentle squeeze and walk out the door. I'm proud of her for standing up for herself. I just hope that she gets the answers she's seeking. That her mother comes clean from all the lies and deceit. After starting her car, I send her a text with the address to Ridge and Kendall's house and letting her know that I'll meet her there.

Chapter 11

Delaney

My phone vibrates in my hand, and it gives me something else to do besides glare at my mother. I skim over Kent's text before sliding my phone back into my pocket. I want to scream and yell, and I know as mad as I am, I'm not going to be able to prevent that from happening. I'm glad Ridge passed on the invitation and I'm glad that Kenton will be there.

"Ready, sweetie?" I ask my daughter.

"Yes!" She jumps in the air and grins. "I'm gonna make all the cookies."

Taking her hand, I lead us out to my rental. I help her get into her seat, and type the address Kenton sent me into my GPS. My hands grip the wheel as anger courses through me. My daughter chatters in the back seat and doesn't seem to notice I'm a million miles away. My mother, she lied. All these years, we could have been a family. Sure, I don't remember, but maybe I would have. How do we know? I wasn't given the opportunity to see him. He didn't get the opportunity to do the right thing, by me or by our daughter. That was stripped from him, just like it was from me.

I'm livid.

I'm hurt.

I'm disappointed.

How much of my life that she filled in for me is a lie? Is any of it true? How can I trust her now? I can barely stand to look at her. Did my father know? Why did he go along with it? Whose idea was it to keep me from Kent? To keep him from me and his daughter? There are a million questions swirling in my mind.

"Momma." Kendrix huffs.

Glancing into the rearview mirror, I see her watching me. "Are we there yet?" she asks, annoyance in her tone.

"Hey, now, is that how we act?" I ask, my eyes back on the road.

"You were 'noring me."

"*Ig*noring. And I wasn't. Not on purpose. Mommy was just lost in thought."

"You're not posta be stracted when driving, Momma."

"*Di*stracted. I know, and I'm sorry. We're almost there. Two minutes is what the GPS says."

"I love making cookies," she tells me.

"I know you do."

"If Mr. Kent is there, I'll teach him like he teached me."

"Like he taught you, and that sounds like a great idea." I'm sure Kenton knows how to make cookies, but something tells me that if Kendrix wanted to teach him, he would pretend otherwise just to have her attention. I should be nervous about leaving my child with people I've just met, but I'm not. In fact, I feel as though she's safer with them than with my mother. My own flesh and blood.

I hate to think that I almost let my mother convince me to just sell the estate, or to let the lawyer, Mr. Garcia, handle everything as far as renovations go. Would I have ever remembered? Would I have ever found out she was lying to me? I swallow back the tears when I think about Kendrix never knowing her daddy. Those two... they're going to be best friends; I can already tell. There's so much for Kenton and me to discuss and work out, but we're taking it one day at a time. First, cookies, then a talk with my mother. Tomorrow, we'll have the test done, and in a few days, we will have hard, concrete poof of her paternity.

As soon as I pull into the driveway, Kendrix starts mumbling about letting her out of her seat. I park next to Kenton's truck, and he appears beside me, opening my door. "Hey, Laney," he says softly. It's a complete contrast to his appearance. He appears to be a hard badass with all the ink and muscles, but to me, and to our daughter, to his friends, and their children, I've only ever seen him be the softie that he is. I don't believe Kenton Baldwin has a mean bone in his entire body.

"Mr. Kent!" Kendrix yells through the car window.

"Can I?" he asks me.

I nod.

He smiles.

My heart flips over in my chest.

I watch as he opens the door, and unstraps her seat as if he's done it hundreds of times. Then again, maybe he has. He does have several nieces and nephews running around. He surprises me when he lifts her from the car and settles her on his hip. My little girl, our little girl grins widely. Being carried is a luxury for her; she's too big for me to pack her around all the time. Kenton, he lifts her as if she weighs nothing.

"Tell Mommy goodbye." He leans into me, letting her give me a hug before jerking her away with a bounce, making her laugh. He does it again, and this time lets her get her arms around me in a hug through her giggles.

"Take care of her," I tell him, suddenly extremely emotional that I'm leaving the two of them here. I want to be here for this.

"What's wrong?" he asks immediately, sensing my hesitation.

"I just... wish I was staying."

"Then stay. We want Mommy to make cookies with us, don't we, kiddo?" he asks her.

Kendrix bobs her little head up and down. "We can teached you."

"Teach," I correct her.

"The whole purpose was to talk to Mom without—" I nod toward Kendrix.

"Just come in for a few minutes. Let yourself see where she's going to be and what we're going to be doing. Then you can go. I can bring her home, or you can come back. Whichever you think is best."

"She has to have a car seat."

"I know. I have one."

"What?"

"I have one."

"When did you find time to order a car seat?"

"Amazon. Two-day shipping. It was at the house last night when I got home."

"I... I don't know what to say to that."

"There is nothing to say. I wanted to be able to help with her and have her with me, and I needed her to be safe." He shrugs like it's not a big deal.

It's a big damn deal.

Huge.

So huge, in fact, I want nothing more than to kiss him. With our daughter in his arms, both of them smiling down at me, that's what I want. More than that, I want this life. I want a partner, someone who can share the good and the bad.

"Come on, Momma, cookies," Kendrix urges me.

"Okay." I smile at her. Reaching into the car, I shut off the engine and close the door. I trail behind the two of them while sending my mother a text message, which she hates.

> **Me:** Going to be a little longer than I thought. Decided to stay for a little while.
>
> **Mom:** This is nonsense, Delaney. Both of you come back here so we can discuss what you think you might know.
>
> **Mom:** How can you believe a complete stranger?

I ignore her and slide my phone in my back pocket. I know her. She's had time to think about this, and we no longer have an audience. It's just me, and when my pocket vibrates four times in a row, I continue to ignore her and her rant.

"Let's make some cookies," Kenton calls out as we enter the house.

"Uncle Kent!" Knox and Everly come running.

If you're impressed that I remembered their names, don't be. Last night, when Kenton dropped me off, I had him go through each of them and their kids' names so I could learn them. I made a note on my phone. I want to be a part of his life, his family, and messing up names and parents isn't a good way to start. He assured me I was putting too much pressure on myself and that it would all work out with time. However, the need to know each of them, to be an active participant in his life, in *their* lives is strong.

Walking into Kendall and Ridge's home, seeing how warm and inviting it is, seeing the kids run and play… it's just like last night at Seth and Mara's. My mother would have a field day with this—she always complains if Kendrix gets too rowdy. She's a kid, that's kind of her job. Anyway, I know that what he said is right. I'm acting like my mother putting too much pressure on myself. That's not how I want to live the rest of my life. That's *not* how I'm going to live the rest of my life.

"Hey, are you ready to make some cookies?" he asks them.

"What's your name?" Knox looks up at Kendrix.

"Kendrix."

Kenton bends down to set her on her feet, and Knox holds his hand out for her and then to his little sister. "If you don't know how to do it, I can show you. My mommy showed me how lots of times."

"My mommy did too." I hear my daughter answer as they disappear into the kitchen.

As soon as they are out of sight, Kenton pulls me into a hug. "I've been dying to do this all day," he says as my phone vibrates in my pocket. At this point, I've lost track of her messages. "What's that?"

"My mother. I'm just going to go. I can't put this off, and she's not going to stop blowing up my phone until I'm home."

"Okay. You sure you don't want me to come with you? She'll be fine here."

"No. I don't want you in the crossfire. I'll call you though. I might have you bring her home, if that's okay?"

"Anything you need. Come say goodbye."

He leads me to the kitchen with his hand on the small of my back. Kendall and Ridge already have all three kids at the island, sleeves rolled up, and ready to bake. "Kendrix, Mommy's gonna run home and talk to Grams for a while. Will you be okay here?"

"Yep." She grins and doesn't seem to have a care in the world except for baking cookies.

I catch Kendall's eyes. "Thank you," I mouth. She winks and turns her attention back to the kids.

"Kendrix," Kent says her name, and she looks up. "I'm going to walk Mommy out to her car. I'll be right back."

"Okay." She nods and goes right back to listening to what Kendall was telling her about taking turns stirring.

At the door, I stop Kenton from going outside. "It's fine. The car is still warm. I'll call you later. Thank you for this. For watching her."

"She's my daughter, Delaney."

I nod. What else is there to say to that? I stand on my tiptoes and kiss his cheek, and then I'm gone. Headed back to my house. To my mother. I'm not looking forward to this conversation, but it has to happen.

Yay me.

I find my mother sitting in the living room, her phone in hand. She looks up and sighs dramatically. It's comical—the show she's putting on. She's already admitted to what she did, without actually doing so. She can't take that back.

"Finally. I thought something had happened to you."

"I told you I was going to be longer than I thought, and that was maybe five minutes. Why the dramatics, Mother?"

"You don't know those people. I told you, this town, it's—" she starts, but I hold my hand up to stop her.

"I don't want to hear you spew some bullshit made-up drama. This town has been nothing but welcoming to me. And those people, that *man,* in particular, he's treated me like gold. Why did you do it, Mother? Why did you lie to me about Kenton?" I won't play her games. We need to cut straight to the heart of this. Maybe we can hash this out. She can give me her bullshit excuse, and I can get back to Kenton and Kendrix and help them with the cookies.

"I—" she starts, but the look in my eyes must tell her that her time for bullshit is up. "You're too good for him."

"What makes you think that?"

"He's small town. I knew it right away. No way would he ever leave this hick life, and you are destined for great things."

"Oh, really? You mean living with you, raising my daughter under your roof, with your rules? Or maybe the great things you're referring to is the lie I've been living. The one you told me about Kenton. About how he told me to get rid of the baby. How he didn't want either of us. How about that lie, Mother? Is that my destiny? Is that the great 'things' you're talking about? Me living a lie. All of us living a lie?"

"All those tattoos, he's a heathen," she deflects.

"He didn't have all of those tattoos back then."

She pales. "You remember?"

"No. But he has pictures of us together." Really only one, but with the lies she's told me, this one isn't even on the map. "And I like the ink. It's sexy."

She gasps. "Delaney Nottingham, I raised you better than to talk like that."

I throw my head back and laugh. "Talk like what? About sex? I'm an adult, Mother. Contrary to what you like to believe. There are no little ears in sight. Just two women having a conversation.'"

"It's trashy."

"And lying to your only daughter after waking up with amnesia, what's that? Huh? How about telling her the man she loved didn't want her? Or depriving your only grandchild of a father who would have loved her, doted on her. On both of us? What about that granddaughter's other grandparents and extended family? Huh? What about all of those people? You robbed every single one of us of years. Kendrix doesn't know her father because of you. *You!*" I scream, feeling tears of frustration prick my eyes.

"How do you know you loved him?"

I just can't with her. "Because I feel it." I place my hand over my chest. "I can't explain it, and I know it sounds crazy, but I feel it. I loved him. And this week, he's been nothing but amazing. And he wants to be in her life. He didn't even want a paternity test. He claimed her as his instantly. He took responsibility, wanted to meet her, wants to be in her life. He loves her already."

"I raised you better than to believe random words from a stranger."

I shake my head. I'm not getting anywhere with her on this, and I'm not going to. She's never going to see the error in her ways. Moving forward, I have to decide what's best for me and my daughter. Regardless of what memories I have, I have to make the choice for me, and for Kendrix. "He's more than a stranger, Mother, and you know it. He was once and who knows, maybe he will be again." I say maybe, but I can already feel it. The connection we have. I feel like I've always known him. I just wish I could remember it.

I turn toward the door, and she grabs my arm, her hand gripping my coat. "Where are you going?"

"Out."

"You can't just leave me here."

"Really, Mother? How old are you? I'm going. Kendrix and I will be home later. And just so you know, we're having a paternity test done. Not on his insistence but on mine. And when the results come back, when I have the hard evidence in black and white, she will know her father."

"Delaney, no." She gasps like I've just told her I'm dying.

"And when she asks me why? When she asks me why she's just now meeting her daddy, what should I tell her? That her grandmother is a lying, conniving piece of work, who kept him from us? That she told us lies about my past to keep us in her pocket? Do you have any ounce of remorse for your action?"

"I was protecting you. Both of you."

"From what? From a man who loved me, who loves her? From being happy. You wanted control, and like a fool, I gave it to you. I was beaten down, depressed from my loss of memory, and I trusted you to guide me. Guess what, *Tillie?*" I ask, using her name. "You lost that trust, you lost a daughter and a granddaughter. This is my home, and you're not welcome here."

"Where am I supposed to go?"

"You're the almighty lady of knowledge. Figure it out. I don't want you here when I get back."

"Delaney, you don't mean that."

"Don't I? I can't stand to look at you or be around you. I'll be damned if I have you around my daughter, poisoning her mind about her father for no other reason than he's not what you wanted for me. He's not some high society jackass. He's a man. A good man with a heart of gold, and he's going to be in our lives. I don't know in what capacity, but I can only hope that somehow through this shitstorm you've caused, I can find my way back to him." With that, I walk out the door, slamming it behind me.

Chapter 12

KENT

The cookies are in the oven, and the kids quickly grew bored of waiting. Knox ran off to play with his trucks, while Everly and Kendrix stayed with the adults. Ridge has Everly curled up on his lap and me, well, I'm holding my little girl. She followed us into the living room and crawled up on my lap like it was the most normal thing in the world for her to do. She's sitting still just watching, as is Everly.

Kendrix sits up and places her hands on my cheeks.

"What's up, sweetheart?"

"Is that her daddy?" She drops her hands and points to Everly and Ridge.

I swallow hard, hoping to dislodge the lump that sits in my throat, but it's still there. I don't know where this conversation is going to go, but I don't want to lie to her. I also promised Delaney I would wait for the results, and I vowed to myself to never lie to her again. "Yes, that's her daddy."

"Oh, my daddy isn't here."

You hear that? That's the sound of my heart cracking wide open. "Everyone has a daddy."

"But he's not here."

There's a knock at the door. Kendall calls out that she'll get it, and a minute later, I hear her voice. Delaney is here. I exhale, not realizing that I was holding my breath, worried about this conversation.

"Looks like everyone is nice and relaxed." She steps into the room, taking the seat next to me.

I might look relaxed on the outside, but inside, I'm shaking. I'm a wreck over the words of my daughter. *My daddy isn't here.*

"Did you have fun making cookies?" she asks Kendrix.

"I did. They haft to cool down."

Her eyes find mine. "You okay?" I ask her.

"Yeah." She leans her shoulder into mine. "I'm okay."

There's something different about her. She almost seems… lighter, as if the load she's been carrying on her shoulders has been lifted.

"Uncle Kent," Everly says, pulling me out of my thoughts. She's standing in front of me, holding a book. "Read story?" she asks, handing it to me.

"Sure, climb on up." I offer her my hand, but she doesn't take it. Instead, she pulls herself up on the couch and burrows into my side. I shift Kendrix so that I have one hand free, and open the book. I read them every page of *Today I'll Be A Princess* and they give me their undivided attention.

"All right, Ev." Ridge stands as I close the book. "It's time for you to get your bath and get in bed."

"You too, sweetie," Delaney tells our daughter.

"I don't wanna go." She juts out her bottom lip in a pout, and I'm ready to ask Ridge if the three of us can camp out here on his couch just to see her smile.

"Well, it's time for bed. How about we have Everly and Knox over to our house for a playdate?"

"Now?" she asks, her voice low and pitiful, as if she can't fathom the thought of leaving.

104

"Not now," Delaney tells her. "How about this weekend?" She looks up at Kendall. "Saturday afternoon?"

"Sounds good to us," Kendall says brightly.

"All right, kiddo. Let me slide you over to Mommy so I can go start our cars."

"No." She throws her arms around my neck and refuses to let go.

"Hey." I rub her back soothingly. "I'll be right back. I promise. How about you walk to the door with me, and you can watch me out the window? It's too cold outside, so we have to start our cars so we can stay warm." She doesn't reply, so I look over at Delaney for help. She has tears in her eyes, but there is a small smile playing at her lips. I mouth, "Help," and her grin grows wider.

"How about I go start the cars?" Delaney offers. She stands, not giving me a chance to object. "Keys in it?" she asks.

"Yes."

She nods, gives my leg a gentle squeeze, and disappears out of the room. It's then that I notice that Ridge, Kendall, and Everly have left the room. I hear them talking upstairs.

"Kendrix, are you excited about your playdate this weekend?"

She pulls away and looks up at me. Her blue eyes are big and beautiful, just like her mother's. "Will you come too? Can we show them how to hammer nails?"

"Is that what you want?"

"Uh-huh. We can show them how you teached me."

"How I taught you," I correct her.

"Yeah, that," she agrees and I chuckle.

How is it that this little angel already has my heart in the palm of her hand? "Okay, sweetheart. I'll stock up and we can show them. Although, their daddy might have already shown them."

"Oh."

"We can still play and have fun. There are lots of things that we can do."

"I wish my daddy was here."

I can't speak. If I do, I'll tell her that I'm right here and that I'm never leaving her again. Never. She goes to college, I'm going too. She gets married, make sure you have a room for Dad, because never again will I ever leave my little girl. I hug her to my chest, trying to comfort her the best that I can.

"Sweetie, time to get your coat." Delaney's voice pulls us out of our cuddle session.

"O-kay." She sighs and climbs off my lap.

I watch them together—mother and daughter. Their routine's so familiar, their language—nonverbal—speaks volumes as they work to get Kendrix into her coat and shoes. I envy the relationship they have.

"You ladies ready to go?" I ask, standing from the couch.

"Mr. Kent, are you coming home with us?" Kendrix looks up at me, her eyes wide with excitement.

I crouch down to her level. "No, I have to go home, but remember about my test tomorrow? You're still going to do it with me, right?"

"Yes! Can we have ice cweam after? My mommy always lets me have it when I go to the doctor." She looks up at Delaney. "Mommy, we have to get ice cweam."

Delaney smiles down at us. "We can definitely make that happen."

"You heading out?" Ridge appears beside us.

"Yeah. Thank you for having us."

"I had lots of fun making cookies," Kendrix says.

"Good. We'll have to do it again sometime."

"Mr. Kent is going to teached us to build with hammers and nails."

"He is?" Ridge feigns excitement. "That sounds like a good time."

"Do they know how to do that?"

"They do, but you want to know a secret?" he asks her.

"I'm good at those," she replies, making him chuckle.

"Even if you already know, practicing is very important."

She looks at me, where I'm still crouched down in front of her. "Hear that? We have to pwactice."

"I heard him." I tap my finger to the end of her nose and stand. "I'll see you in the morning," I tell Ridge.

"Sounds good." He waves, and we turn to leave.

Delaney opens the door, and Kendrix turns to me with her hands held up in the air. "Carry me."

I don't waste any time bending and scooping her up in my arms and settle her on my hip. She throws her arms around my neck and we're off. I help her into her seat in the back of the Durango. "I'll see you in the morning for our test. And if Mommy says it's okay, we can go to the store tomorrow night and get more building sets."

"Yay. Bye." She waves.

I force myself to pull away from her and shut the door.

"You spoil her, you know. She's going to have you carrying her all over the place."

"I'm good with that. I owe her a few."

"No." She rests her palm against my cheek and steps into me. I snake my arm around her waist, holding her close. "You don't owe us anything, Kenton. You didn't do anything wrong. You made a mistake, one you tried to correct, but my mother, she conspired against you."

"How did it go?"

"She didn't deny it. I told her to leave. I can't stand to look at her right now."

"I'm sorry, Laney."

"Don't be. I'm sorry. She kept us from you, and you missed out on things that you will never get back. I can't tell you how sorry I am for that."

"We look toward to the future."

"Yeah, what does that look like?"

"I'm not exactly sure, but I do know that it's the three of us together."

"Yeah?"

I nod. "Drive safe, babe. Call me when you get home?"

"I will. You too." Her hand falls away and she retreats, forcing me to release my hold on her. I step back and wait for her to get behind the wheel and drive away. I don't notice the cold, or the snow that starts to fall—just her taillights disappearing into the night. I hate that they're driving away from me. I look forward to the day that we're both headed in the same direction. To the same house. To the same bed. The odds of our past are against us, but our hearts and our future are front and center.

My phone rings just as I'm walking through the door. A quick glance at the screen tells me it's Delaney. "Hey, you," I greet her.

"Hey. We're home." I can hear the irritation in her voice.

"What's wrong?"

"Nothing." She sighs.

"Delaney."

"Fine. She's still here. Apparently, she thought I didn't mean what I said. I just… hate the thought of being around her right now. I hate that Kendrix is around her. She stole so much from us."

"Come here. Or I can come there and make her leave. Call the cops, something."

"Don't tempt me, but I can't call the cops on her. No matter how much I wish that I could."

"Then come here. Pack a bag for you and Kendrix and come and stay with me."

"The renovations, and then the tests are tomorrow."

"Ridge and the guys can handle themselves, trust me. I'll take the day off, and the three of us can spend it together."

"What about the tests?" She didn't toss out my spending the day together. Not yet.

"I have the number for the tech who's coming in the morning. I can call him and tell him to come here. It's not an issue."

"It's so soon, and I don't know. I just… I don't want to be here with her."

"I have a spare room. The two of you can sleep there, or better yet, take my room and my king-size bed. I'll take the spare. I want you here, Laney. Both of you. Please. I hate that you're there and miserable. Please come and stay with me." I'm not above begging her to get them here. I hated leaving them, and this is the answer to that.

"Thank you, Kent." She shortens my name, and although small, it means that she feels more comfortable with me. I'll take all the small victories I can get. "We're not in danger. I just can't stand looking at her. I appreciate your offer, but right now, I don't think that's a good idea. I believe you when you say she's yours. I see it, but until we know, until we tell her, I don't think it's a good idea that she and I stay with you."

My shoulders deflate, and the hope I had of spending more time with them, of having them here with me where they belong, collapses. "I understand. Doesn't mean I like it."

"I'm sorry."

"Hey." I soften my voice. "There is nothing for you to be sorry for. You're innocent in all of this. Can you promise me something?"

"Yes." There is zero hesitation in her reply.

"Will you come to me? If things get bad there, if you and Kendrix need to get away, you come to me. Let me be the place you run to."

"My mother doesn't fight. She's the silent-treatment type. But I promise you, if we need you, if anything changes, it will be you I call."

"Good. Now kiss our daughter goodnight for me, and get some rest."

"Goodnight, Kent."

Turning off the lights, and making sure the door is locked, I head to my room. Stripping down, I slide under the covers and let my mind wander to what it would be like if she were here in my arms. Kendrix sleeping just down the hall. Hell, she could be in this bed with us for that matter. I know they say not to let kids do that because they get used to it, but that's babies, right? I just want them both close to me all the time. Eventually, exhaustion takes over as I drift off to sleep, dreaming of my angels.

Chapter 13

Delaney

It's Saturday early afternoon, and I don't think I've stopped smiling since Kent called me this morning. Even after the shitshow of a day yesterday, I can't keep the smile off my face.

My mother was here when the tech came for the test, and she threw a fit. Stomping around saying I was ridiculous to trust a stranger. Kendrix had a meltdown, because Gram was upset and didn't want her to take the test. I was on the verge of a breakdown when Mara showed up. Apparently, she was delivering a tool the guys left at the shop, but as soon as I saw her, she could tell something was up. Call it women's intuition or hell, call it pure luck, but she rushed to me, wrapped her arms around my shoulders, and told me it was all going to be okay.

A stranger, a woman I've met once, could see what the day was doing to me and offered me words of encouragement and comfort. I gave her a quick rundown of the morning and apologized for her seeing me distraught, and she laughed, telling me that was life, and I had nothing to be sorry for. The next thing I know, she's got my mother in the kitchen, yammering on about her dress, and California. I went off to look for Kendrix and found her just where she needed to be.

With her daddy.

Kent was sitting on the bed with her in his arms, explaining that sometimes adults say things they don't mean, and that Grammy loved her and was having a bad day. The man is a damn saint.

Anyway, the tech did the test on Kent first as Kendrix watched. He made a big deal out of it, saying it tickled, making her laugh. Like the superstar she is, our little girl opened wide and let the tech swab her cheek and just like that, the crisis was averted.

Mother was pissed. I'm not even sure that's an accurate description, but the outcome was one we all needed. She flew home yesterday afternoon with the promise that as soon as I came to my senses, she would be back.

Yesterday was crazy and stressful, but then this morning, Kent called first thing asking if he could invite the other kids over for the playdate. Of course I said yes, and that leads us to now. My house is filled with Kent's inner circle and their children. The wives brought in Crock-Pots of soup, and meatballs, and I'm not sure what else is in the kitchen. I made brownies and was just going to order pizza. This is so much better than that. I need to get this kitchen stocked if we're going to be doing more of this.

I hope we do more of this.

"You okay?" Kent asks, stepping up beside me. His hand settles on the small of my back, his body angled toward me. My entire being tingles with his touch as the warmth of his skin heats my back.

"Yes." I smile at him. "I'm more than okay. This is…. I love it for her. We don't have this back home in California." I turn my attention to the room filled with people who are here getting to know one of their own's daughter. When Kent called me this morning and asked if everyone could come, he followed it up with "I want my people to meet my daughter and the incredible woman who brought her to me." How was I supposed to say no to that?

"She's having a good time. They all are. Thank you for letting us invade your house."

"We have the space, and how could I deny you this?"

"You having fun?"

"Yes. Your friends are great."

"They're my family, Laney. I know you don't remember, but I never introduced you to them. That first night at the bar, you met them, but after that, I kept you locked up. Just for me. I don't know why I did it, but I did. I can't tell you how sorry I am for that."

I shrug. "I don't remember it. Any of it. You could lie and tell me we were all the best of friends."

"I vowed to never lie to you again. I told you I would meet you, and I did, but I was hours late, and you left. I never saw you again, you had our baby and I didn't know. Never again will I ever break a promise to you, lie to you, and you can damn sure bet you'll never be a secret again."

"You're talking like this is a sure thing. Me and you."

"A man can dream. Besides, regardless of what happens between us, I'm her father. We're going to be in each other's lives and that vow, those promises, they still exist. No matter our relationship, you can count on that."

"I wish I could remember," I say softly.

"I know, baby. Me too," he says, his voice just as soft.

His eyes sparkle as the endearment slips from his lips, and my heart swells. Kenton Baldwin in an incredible man. I hope with everything in me that he is indeed the father of my daughter. I pray we're both right and that my little girl will have the presence of this man in her life.

"Momma!" Kendrix climbs to her feet and rushes toward us. Kent drops his hand from the small of my back, our moment lost but not forgotten. "Can we stay here forever and ever?" she asks, smiling up at me. Her blue eyes are shining with delight that only a child can carry, unaware of the hatred in the world.

"That's a long time." I chuckle.

Her little head bobs up and down while she bounces on her toes, unable to stand still. "It's so fun, and so many friends." She stops bouncing and looks at Kent. "Come on, Mr. Kent, we have to hammer." She grabs his hand and begins to tug.

He follows along with her easily, letting her pull him wherever her little heart desires. He looks back at me and winks. "Forever and ever." He grins before turning his attention back to our daughter.

"You're good for him."

Turning, I see Reagan standing next to me. "It's messy."

She laughs. "Life is messy." She goes on to tell me about Knox's mother, the heart condition of one of her twins, how Dawn and Mark ended up adopting Daisy, and Seth and Mara's story, the loss of their beloved friend, and baby Ryder. I listen to everything this group of friends has gone through, and I understand even more why Kent refers to them as his family. "So you see," Reagan says, "we get messy. It's not something you can avoid, but love, love is something you can't avoid, and that man, he's done everything in his power to look the other way."

"What do you mean?"

"He's never been serious with anyone. Never. Hell, the last few years, he's not even dated that I'm aware of. We're all pretty tight. The guys always have been, but after Knox was born and Kendall was brought into the fold, and my sweet baby nephew, that group expanded. It's no longer just the guys, but the wives and kids as well. They've all fallen, and to be honest, I wasn't sure Kent ever would."

"Why do you say that?" I ask, my heart racing. My palms are sweaty as I stand here and learn things about the man who, from what I'm told, I was close to all those years ago.

"He's always been holding back. He's happy, loves his nieces and nephews, is always there if we need him, no matter what, but there's still been this… quietness about him. It's hard to explain, but I thought it was worth mentioning."

"Can I ask why? Why mention it now? To me?" I'm confused about what she's trying to tell me. She's being cryptic in a sense, and I can't seem to figure out where she's going with all of this.

"I mention it now because it's gone. The quietness is gone. There's nothing there but a full heart and eyes full of hope."

"Oh."

She smiles. "Yeah, and you want to know when things changed for him?"

I can't speak, and even if I could, I'm afraid my reply wouldn't be friendly. I don't need to know, and I don't want to know. Not if it means that he's moved on. Is that what she's saying? He says differently, but damn it, what do I know? How do I know who to trust? This is all so messed up.

"The moment he found you again. You're good for him. I hope you're thinking about sticking around. We'd miss him, and we just lost a member of our family. I don't know that we can go through that again."

"What? Is he sick?"

"No, Delaney, but he's a good man. If you leave here, if you go back to California, he's going to follow you. And when I say follow you, I don't mean to visit. I mean, he's going to leave here and go with you."

"This is his home." Surely, he wouldn't just pack up and leave just like that. Would he?

She points to where Kent is sitting on the floor with Kendrix in his lap. "She's his home, his heart, and her momma too. Just... consider your options and his. What each of you would be leaving behind."

"We don't have the results back yet," I say, trying to stall my mind from going into overdrive to decipher our conversation.

"We don't need them to know the truth. He's adamant, and she looks like him. She's the perfect mix of the two of you. You all make pretty babies," she teases.

"Look at them." Mara joins us with baby Ryder in her arms. "A bunch of softies." She motions to where the men are sitting in a circle, kids on their laps as they play with building blocks.

"He's adorable," I say, reaching out to run my index finger on the top of Ryder's little hand.

"Thank you. He's our miracle baby." She stares down at her son.

Had Reagan not filled me in, I wouldn't have understood that statement, but I get it. The bond of this group is unlike anything I've ever experienced.

"Would one of you mind holding him? I need to use the restroom."

"Babe!" Tyler calls out. "We need help." He points to one of his sons and waves his hand in front of his face.

"We're still potty training. Looks like I have an accident to attend to." Reagan rushes off to help her husband.

"I'll take him." I hold my arms out for Mara to transfer Ryder to me. "Oh, my. It's been a long time since I've held a little one. Hello, handsome." I smile down at him. He's wide awake, looking all around and taking in this raucous bunch.

I make my way to the other side of the living room and settle on the couch. Ryder and I snuggle. "What do you think about all of this, little man? Won't be long and you'll be joining in on all the fun."

"God, what I wouldn't give to be able to go back and see you like this with her, with our little girl." Kent takes a seat next to me on the couch.

"Where's Kendrix?" I glance up and at the group.

"She's showing Kendall and Everly her birdhouse in her room." He leans in and taps Ryder's chin and he wiggles his little arms and legs, obviously recognizing his uncle Kent.

"I hate that you missed it all. We missed out too, you know. We could have had you all this time."

"You want more?" Kent nods to the baby in my arms.

I nod in response. "Although I wasn't sure it would even happen for me again. My life has revolved around Kendrix for so long. Between her and finishing my final year of college one class at a time, and working full-time as an independent graphic designer, there's not exactly a lot of time to meet someone."

"That's the universe's way of telling you you've already met him. It brought you here to me."

"Do you smooth talk all the women like this?"

"What women?" He raises his eyebrows, challenging me.

"You know, the women you date."

"We've talked about this. There hasn't been anyone for me since you."

"Surely you've, you know, hooked up, had a one-night stand, whatever."

"Nope."

"How is that possible?"

"I've dated, flirted, drove a couple of girls home from the bar, but I never slept with any of them."

"What? Come on now. What happened to all that honesty stuff you were spewing at me? Does today not count? Or are you already dropping the ball on that one?" I regret the words as soon as they are out of my mouth. "I'm sorry," I rush to add. "That was uncalled for. I'm just…

you're a lot to take in, Kenton Baldwin, and this is intense. *You're intense.*"

"I made a vow to you and to myself and now to our daughter. All of me, 100 percent open and honest, no matter what. I won't risk losing you again over something stupid."

"I don't live here," I state the obvious, but Reagan's little chat has been rolling over and over in my mind since I sat down.

"I know. We'll figure it out."

"What does that mean?"

"It means we will figure it out. Together."

I don't press him for more. Honestly, I don't know if I'm ready for his truth serum. We just need to get past the next few days and get these results. The more time I spend with him, the more I want to. In the back of my mind, there is "what if." What if we're wrong? What if he's not her father? Then what? There will be more pain for him, and for me. The fewer plans we make, the better off we are. Just in case.

What are the odds that fate brought us together? Then again, was it fate or my father? I block it out as best as I can and just try to enjoy the moments—all of the moments, soaking them up like a sponge. Regardless of what those results say, Kenton Baldwin is not a man you ever forget. I know I will never in my lifetime ever meet anyone like him, so I'm taking all the moments I can get and storing them away. Just in case.

Chapter 14

KENT

Today has been one I'll never forget. Not ever. And tonight, well, it's one for the books too. After everyone left, I stayed behind. I couldn't seem to leave them. Kendrix asked me to watch a movie with her, and no way could I tell my little girl no. Delaney took care of pulling it up on her laptop and handed it to me. I took a seat on the couch, and Kendrix, she crawled right up on my lap and snuggled close to see the screen. When she called for her momma to come watch, well, that's how we ended up where we are now.

My back is against the arm of the couch, Kendrix is on my lap and Delaney is snuggled in close to my side. We're watching the movie on a laptop, so yeah, we have to be close in order to see it. Not that I'm complaining. I slipped my arm around Delaney's shoulders about twenty minutes ago without reservation or complaint from her, and Kendrix, I'm holding her with the other. I have both my girls in my arms where they belong. So, as amazing as today was, with all my friends here, with my girls. Tonight, it's just for us, and it's not only a moment I will never forget but one I will cherish until the day I take my last breath.

"Again," Kendrix says sleepily as the credits roll.

"No can do, little lady. It's bedtime."

"No. I'm not tired," she says as she covers a yawn with her hand.

"Hey, I was thinking. I'd like to take you and your mommy somewhere tomorrow. Somewhere really special. How does that sound?"

"We go now?" she asks.

"No, sweetheart. We have to get a good night's sleep so we can go tomorrow."

"Okay," she concedes easily enough. "Will you read me a story?"

My chest tightens and a lump forms in my throat. "Yes," I croak.

"Kendrix, why don't you go get some jammies on and we'll be there in a minute."

"Don't forget, Mr. Kent," she tells me as she jumps off my lap and rushes down the hall.

"I-I couldn't tell her no. I'm sorry. I know you didn't want me—I couldn't tell her no."

"It's fine. There's no harm in you reading a bedtime story."

I nod, suddenly nervous. I've done this reading gig to my nieces and nephews so many times, but tonight, it's different. It's more. It's my little girl I'm going to be reading to. This is surreal, and really hits home that I'm a father. She's a part of me, and always will be. That's... incredible.

"Mr. Kent!" Kendrix yells out for me. "I'm weady."

I smile. "I'll be back, or do you want to come too?" I stand from the couch and ask Delaney.

"No. You go ahead." She doesn't say it, but I can see it in her eyes she's giving me this moment. This special time with our daughter.

Leaning down, I place a kiss on the corner of her mouth. It's the closest I've come to actually kissing her, and although I want that, I crave that connection with her, it's going to have to wait. Not just because my little girl is waiting for me, but she needs to see it in writing. Delaney doesn't remember, and she's been told so many things, she needs to see it. I know she says she believes me, but she needs that hard evidence that what I say is true. Once we get that, all bets are off. I'm not staying away from either of them. I want them both in my life. Permanently.

With each step I take that carries me down the hall, the more nervous I become. My palms are sweating, and my knees, they're a bit wobbly as I stand in the doorway of her room. The overhead light is off, and there is a dim glow from the bedside lamp. "Somebody need a bedtime story?" I ask.

"Me." She raises her hand. "Come lay with me."

Slowly, my feet carry me to the side of the bed. It's a queen or maybe a full, and she's so tiny sitting there all by herself. "This is a big bed for such a little girl."

She giggles. "I love it. My grammy said it was extwa when she lived here."

"Extra," I correct her.

"That's what I said." She nods as if I need her agreement to believe her. "Lay with me." She scoots over and pats the bed next to her.

Not needing to be told twice, I climb on the bed and rest my back against the headboard. She curls up next to me, resting her head on my chest, and we start to read. I change my voice, which makes her giggle, and I read slow, never wanting this moment to end. When I finally reach the last page, I look down, and she's sound asleep. Without thinking, I press my lips to the top of her head and then carefully slide out from under her. I sit on the side of the bed and watch her sleeping. She's peaceful and looks like a little angel. I don't know how long I sit here and watch her sleep, but my phone vibrating in my pocket pulls me out of my trance.

Standing slowly, not wanting to make too much movement and wake her up, I pull my phone from my pocket and look at the screen. It's a text message from Reagan. Clicking it, I see an image of Kendrix and me from earlier today. She's sitting on my lap looking up at me. Her head is tilted back and we're both smiling. In the background is Delaney. She's watching us with a small smile playing on her lips, and the look in her eyes, it's… longing? Hopeful?

Sliding my phone back into my pocket, I lean over and kiss Kendrix on the forehead. "Night, baby girl." *Daddy loves you.* Soon. I'll be able to say those words soon. Turning off the bedside lamp, I creep out of her room, pulling the door almost closed, leaving it open just a crack in case she needs something. I want Delaney to be able to hear her. I move to start down the hall and startle when I see Delaney sitting on the floor.

Her back is against the wall, and her knees are bent, her arms hugging them to her chest as her head rests against them.

I take a seat next to her, stretching my long legs as far as they'll go in this small hallway. "What's going on?"

She's quiet for several long minutes before turning her head to look at me. There are tears in her eyes. "This is all so… overwhelming, Kenton." She's back to using my full name. "How could my mother have done this? And worse, what if all that you're saying is true, but you're still not her father? Then what? I can't remember," she says as a tear slides down her cheek. "She is the most precious gift in my life, and I can't remember a single second of her being conceived. And if she's not yours… then… she has to be yours."

"Come here." I put my arm around her shoulders and she leans into me without hesitation. "That's not the kind of person you were, Laney. You were loyal and loving, and you were the best thing to ever happen to me. I know this is hard for you, baby, and I'm trying to remember that you can't, but I promise you that you were not sleeping with anyone else. That's not who you were."

"I hate this. I hate that you have all of these memories of us, and I have this… blank space. I have you in my dreams, holding your hand out to me, but I don't know where you're asking me to go. I hate that we lost you and everything we missed out on."

"I'm sorry." I don't know what else to say. And in reality, I don't think she needs me to say anything. I think she just needs me. I think she needs someone to hold her and let her cry out her frustrations. She needs someone who is on her side, no matter what, and I'm that guy. So we sit here in the hallway outside our daughter's bedroom door, and I hold her while she cries silently into my chest.

I hear a soft giggle, one that sounds like my daughter, and it's too real to be a dream. Peeling my eyes open, I see Kendrix standing in the hallway, a teddy bear in her hands, still wearing her pink princess pajamas. "Morning, princess." The endearment falls from my lips easily.

"Mr. Kent, did you and Mommy have a sleepover?"

I take a minute to survey my current situation to see what she sees. Delaney is lying on the floor with her head on my lap, curled up on her side. I'm in the same position I was in last night—back against the wall, legs bent out in front of me, and I can already feel the ache seep in from sleeping in the same position all night long.

"We fell asleep."

"In the hallway?" She giggles.

Delaney opens her eyes. "Hey, sweetie."

"Momma, you and Mr. Kent had a sleepover."

Delaney jerks to a sitting position, blinks, and takes stock of what our daughter sees. "We uh—" she starts, but I cut her off.

"How about you go brush your teeth and get ready? So I can take you and your mommy to that special place I was telling you about."

"Yay, but my belly is angwy," she says, scrunching up her nose.

I can't stop the chuckle that her words evoke. "We'll stop and pick up breakfast too. Go get ready." She jumps and spins, rushing back into her room.

"Where are we going?"

"First, you get ready. I'm going to run home and grab a quick shower, and then I'll be back to pick you ladies up. Then we're going to make our daughter's belly happy. I promised to take the two of you somewhere special, and I plan to do just that. So, get moving, woman." I tap her leg and pull my stiff body from the floor. I offer her my hand, helping her to stand. She starts to walk down that hall, but I pull her back to me. I cradle her face in my hands and lean in, placing my lips next to her ear. "Morning, beautiful." I kiss her neck and then force myself to step away.

Her smile, it's bright, and her blue eyes are filled with happiness, none of the sadness from last night making an appearance. "Thank you, Kent."

"It's my pleasure, baby. Now go." I point down the hall and watch her until she disappears into her room. I have to force myself to turn away and leave them. Just a few more days until she has my truth in her hands.

Forty-five minutes later, I'm pulling into her driveway. I leave the truck running as I jog to the front door and knock. Delaney opens the door with a smiling Kendrix on her heels. "Hello, ladies. You ready to go?"

"My belly is weally, weally angwy," Kendrix says, pulling her hat on over her ears.

I bend and lift her into my arms. "Well then, we better take care of that angry belly. Momma, you ready to go?" I ask Delaney.

"Yes." She grabs her purse and we step out onto the porch. I bounce down the steps, making my daughter laugh before strapping her into her seat in the back seat of my truck.

Kendrix chatters in the back seat about surprises and how mad her belly is at her. It's the cutest thing I've ever heard. Delaney and I listen to her ramble on, answering her questions when she asks. She's full of energy, even with an empty belly.

"We're here," I say, pulling the truck into the lot of the local diner in town. "This place has the best pancakes around." I turn to look at Kendrix. "Does your belly like pancakes?"

"Yes. And bacon. My belly weally likes bacon."

"This kid." I smile over at Delaney before climbing out of the truck and helping Kendrix out of her seat. "I wanna sit by you," Kendrix announces as we make our way inside.

I glance over at Delaney, and she nods, a small smile playing on her lips. "All right, princess, you can sit by me." We make our way to the back of the restaurant and find a booth.

"Welcome, can I start you off with some drinks?" the waitress asks.

"Milk, please," Kendrix asks politely.

"You know what, milk for me too," I tell her.

"And you, miss?"

"Orange juice, please," Delaney tells her.

"You like milk too?" Kendrix asks.

"I do. I used to drink nothing but milk when I was your age."

"My momma hates it." She sticks her tongue out. "She says it's like eating chalk. Do you like chalk, Mr. Kent? I never had it. My momma says it's bad for you, but that milk is good for you. I don't get it." She shakes her head and furrows her little brow.

"Well, milk is very good for you. It gives you strong bones."

"Yeah, I'll be big like you." She nods and then reaches for the small cup that holds a few crayons and begins to color on her placemat.

Our waitress delivers our drinks, and we all order pancakes with a side of bacon. I teach Kendrix how to play tic-tac-toe and, by the time our food is delivered, we've filled up her placemat and mine. The three of us eat and talk like this is our normal Sunday morning routine. Like we've been doing this for years. Maybe it's a new tradition for us. I can only hope.

"All right, you ladies ready for your surprise?" I ask them once we're back in my truck.

"Yes!" Kendrix cheers, and I feel her kicking her legs around on the back seat of the truck.

I glance over at Delaney. "This one is really for you, but I wanted her to see it too."

She nods but doesn't comment. The ride to the meadow is short. I enter in the back way so my parents don't see us. I haven't told them yet, about my girls. It's not that I don't want to, but if I'm wrong, and my gut tells me I'm not, I don't want to hurt them. My mother has been asking for me to settle down since Knox was born. Funny, if Delaney had still been in my life, Kendrix would have been the firstborn of our little group.

"Here we are," I say, pulling my truck into the middle of the open meadow and putting it in Park.

Delaney glances into the back seat. "She's out."

"Might be a good thing."

"Where are we?"

"This is a spot we used to hang out at. Just the two of us. It's my parents' land. Their house is just through those trees. We used to come out here in the summer, kill the engine and the lights, and sit in the bed of my truck. We'd talk for hours, among other things."

"Other things?" she whispers.

"Yeah. The night we met, we left the bar together, and this is where I brought you. It started pouring down rain, but thankfully, my old truck had a bench seat. It's where I made love to you for the first time."

"Wow."

"I still have it, you know? The truck. It held too many memories to just get rid of it. It's at my parents' place, stored in their old barn. I thought one day I'd restore it to its former glory. It's had a rough life." I chuckle.

"You kept it?" Delaney asks.

"I had to. It was the last piece of anything I had that reminded me of you. I had my memories, but that old truck, it's special. Same reason I've never moved into another place. Every time I walk through the doors at my place, a rush of memories of our time there together assaults me."

"I didn't peg you for the sentimental type."

"Yeah, not usually. Only those moments and the people who are special to me."

"And I'm one of those people?"

"You're at the top of the list, Laney."

She turns her head and gazes out at the meadow. "It's beautiful here."

"Yes. You loved it here. It was always one of your favorite places for me to bring you."

"Do you mind sitting with her?" She motions with her head toward the back seat. "I just need a minute."

"Of course. Take however long you need. Here." I open the center console of my truck and hand her a scarf and a pair of my gloves that are way too big for her but will help ward off the cold weather. She takes them without comment, and once she's bundled up, she's stepping out of my truck and into the frigid air.

I watch her as she takes step after step until she's about fifty feet away from the truck. I can't see her face, but when she tilts her head back, I can imagine that her eyes are closed and she's taking it all in. The fresh air, the memories I've just given her. Maybe, just maybe she's remembering. That's why I brought her here. I was hoping that seeing this place, where we spent all our time, that it would trigger something for her.

I've been reading online, and the brain is a tricky thing. There's a chance she could still one day remember, but that chance is equally as great for her not remembering. I can't imagine what it feels like for her. To have someone tell you what happened in your life, having years gone that you can't recall.

I don't take my eyes off her as she stands and stares out into the distance. I wish I knew what she was thinking. I also wish I could make it better, that I could take this confusion and this pain away from her. The odds have been stacked against us from the beginning.

Glancing at the clock on the dash, I see she's been out there for twenty minutes. She has to be freezing. Unbuckling my seat belt, I turn to look at Kendrix, who is still sleeping peacefully. I climb out of the truck and quietly shut the door to keep from waking her. Slowly, I make my way to Delaney. The closer I get, the easier it is to see her shoulders shaking. I don't know if she's shivering from the cold or—When I hear a sob, I know it's not the cold, but tears that are causing her body to quiver.

As soon as I reach her, I wrap my arms around her, and she buries her face in my chest. "I've got you." I try to soothe her, holding her close and trying to warm her and let her know she's not alone all at the same time.

"It's all so messed up. This place, it's familiar to me."

"Hey," I say soothingly. "That's a good thing."

"No, Kent, you don't understand. This place. It's the same one I dream about every night. You're standing in this exact meadow, with your hand held out for me. Those trees—" She points to the tree line off in the distance. "—they're behind you in my dreams."

I don't know what to say to that, so I don't say anything. Instead, I hold her a little tighter, showing her I'm here. I'm here with her and I'm never leaving her. I don't know what that means for our future, but I do know I won't be away from them, from her or our daughter ever again.

"I hate her. I hate my mother. How could she do this, Kent? How could she tear us apart like that, and Kendrix?" Her voice cracks. "Our sweet baby girl. How could she keep her from her father?" She looks up at me. "She kept us from you."

"I didn't show up," I say, even though she already knows. I'm trying to alleviate some of her anger from her mother to me.

"It doesn't matter. Couples fight, they have disagreements. I never would have kept you from her. Never. I might have been upset, and I might not remember those few years of my life, but I promise you, that's not who I am. I never would have kept our daughter from you. Never," she says again. There's conviction in her tone.

"I know." I kiss the top of her head. "I know you wouldn't have." Pulling back, I place my finger under her chin and lift her eyes to mine. "You don't have to convince me, Laney. I know the kind of woman you are, and I know you've been an incredible mother to our daughter. The situation was out of your control."

"I should have questioned it. Questioned her. And my father? What is his role in all of this? I didn't ask her. I should have, but I was too angry. I just wanted her gone."

"You'll have time to ask her, and who knows, maybe you will never know the answers. Now, we better get back before Kendrix wakes and gets scared that we're not there."

Her hand moves to my cheek and her eyes soften. "You're a good man, Kenton. I don't know if I've told you this, but I've thought it a million times over. I'm glad it was you."

"Me too, baby." Bending, I place a feather-soft kiss to her lips. I know I shouldn't, but I can't help it. She doesn't shy away, and when I walk her to the truck, tucked in close to my side, it feels like old times.

I'm not a betting man, not anymore, but I think although unexpected, the odds are in our favor.

Chapter 15

Delaney

I've been a mess all week. Wondering, waiting, and still nothing. It's Thursday afternoon and although waiting sucks, Kent has done a great job at keeping us occupied. Kendrix is in love with him. She thinks that he hung the moon, and she still has no idea that he's her daddy. When she finds out, she's going to go nuts. In a good way. At least I hope that's the outcome.

The three of us have had dinner every night this week. Monday night it was pizza at the local pizza place in town. Tuesday night we went to a steakhouse. Kendrix got a kick out of the fact that you got to eat peanuts and throw the shells on the floor. Wednesday night, we went through the drive-thru and then drove to the meadow. The three of us ate while watching the sunset. Kendrix sat on the center console and commanded our attention all night, and it was perfect. The three of us, our little family.

At least I hope. Other than my memory to come back, I don't know that I've ever wanted anything more.

Speaking of memory, since Sunday, I've been dreaming the same dream, only I can see the meadow clearly, and this time, I place my hand in his, and we begin to walk off into the open field. Then I wake up. It's more than I've had over the years as the pieces hopefully are starting to fall together. I haven't mentioned it to Kent. I don't want to get his hopes up.

Tonight, we're staying in. Apparently, Kendrix and Kent are going to make spaghetti, which she hasn't stopped talking about all day. I found her in the upstairs bathroom—that the guys are currently working on putting back together. Kent had her in his arms settled on his hip while they talked about noodles and sauce. Seth, he was on the floor laying tile and chiming in on their conversation like it was the most normal thing in the world. It's not just Kent who lets her run around like she's the boss. They all do. It's endearing to see these men with her. After seeing them with her, and their own wives and kids, I know Kendrix and I are lucky to have them in our lives.

The more time I spend here, the more I don't want to leave. It was Mom who wanted me to sell, and I don't want to do that. Kent has been great, not pressuring me for what comes next. I know he's waiting on the results. We both are.

"Laney." His deep timbre pulls me out of my trance.

I set my Kindle down on the couch and stand. "Hey, is it Kendrix? Is she up from her nap? I swear the girl never takes naps these days, but running around this house and trying to keep up with you and the guys seems to wear her out," I ramble.

"Laney," he says again. This time he steps closer. He doesn't stop until we're toe-to-toe. "I just got the call. The results are in. I'm going to drive over to the hospital to get them."

"Th-The results are in?" I stammer.

"Yes."

His expression is well... expressionless. I can't get a read on him. "What are they? What did they say?"

"I don't know. I want us to open them together. I feel as though there are so many moments that we missed out on, and when we open that envelope that tells us that I'm her father, it will kind of be like you telling me you were pregnant. I know it's not the same thing, but it will be a moment. It will be ours."

"I'll come with you."

"No. Kendrix is still sleeping. I have to run to the shop as well and pick up a tool we forgot. We're going to start the demo on the kitchen."

"But dinner, we were making dinner."

"We still can, just at my place. I didn't expect us to be done with the bathrooms until tomorrow. I'll just take you guys home with me, and then bring you back later."

"Okay. So, you're going now?"

"Yes. I'll be back as soon as I can." He opens his mouth to say something else, but quickly closes it. Instead, he leans in and presses his lips to mine, and then he's gone.

Exactly one hour and four minutes later, he's pulling into the driveway. Yes, I counted the minutes. Kendrix is sitting next to me with a glass of milk, and some carrots and ranch dressing. The door swings open, and his dark brown eyes filled with so much emotion find mine. He holds the envelope up and nods.

"Thought that was you," Mark says, coming into the room. "Kendrix, I know you're eating your snack, but I thought you might want to help me with something."

"I'm all done. See." She holds up her empty bowl as she pops the last carrot into her mouth. The ranch dressing starts to run, but I grab the bowl just in time. Not that it matters. We're replacing this carpet anyway. "Momma, can I help Mr. Mark?"

"Just Mark, kiddo, or you can call me Uncle Mark."

"Weally? I don't have an uncle. Wait. What's an uncle?" she asks, making us all laugh.

"Yes, you can go with Mark." I leave off both the Mr. and the uncle for now.

She takes his offered hand, and they disappear into the kitchen.

"Come here, baby." Kent holds his hand out for me, just like Mark did for Kendrix, and just like my daughter, I don't hesitate to place my hand in his. He guides us upstairs and down the hall to the very back bedroom. Once inside, he closes the door and flips the lock. "You ready for this?"

"Are you ready for this is the bigger question? I know she's mine."

"And I know she's mine." He hands me the envelope.

"You don't want to do the honors?" My voice quivers.

"No. I know what it says." He taps his chest right over his heart. "I don't need that piece of paper to tell me what I know, but I have my memories, Laney. You need this. Open it." He holds the letter out again, and this time with shaking hands, I take it from him.

My knees wobble and Kent notices. With his hand on the small of my back, he leads me to the bed. I sit and stare at the white envelope that has Kent's name scrawled across the front.

"I'm right here, Laney. No matter what that piece of paper says, I'm right here."

I nod, letting his words sink in, and turn the envelope over in my hands, sliding my index finger under the seal. Slowly, I pull out the single folded sheet of paper, and take my time, opening each layer. Then, my eyes scan the words, the numbers, and my heart soars.

"She's yours," I say as a sob rips from my chest. My eyes are blurry from tears as I read it once more. 99.9 percent match. Everything Kent has told me is true. Kendrix is his daughter. *Our* daughter.

"I fucking knew it." His strong arms wrap around me. His hold is tight as he rests his forehead on my shoulder. His body shakes and I take a deep breath, trying to calm down, but then I realize that it's not me that's causing it. It's him. Standing from the bed, I turn to stand in front of him, settling between his legs. I wrap my arms around him, his head against my chest. His arms grip around my waist and together, we cry. For what we lost, for what we've gained, and for the future before us.

"Are you okay?" I whisper.

"More than okay. I knew she was mine." He pulls back and peers up at me. "I felt it in my heart that she was my little girl, but there was always that doubt, you know. The odds have been stacked against us since day one, and I was so afraid to think about if I was wrong. What if she wasn't mine, and you took her away from me? What if she wasn't mine and you took *you* away from me?" Reaching up, his hands cradle either side of my face. "You're both mine, Laney. I'll stop at nothing to prove that to you." He pauses, giving me time to process his words. "I loved you." He exhales as if he's been waiting years to say those words to me. And well, I guess he has.

"Did I know that?"

"No." His eyes bore into mine. "I like to think I showed you in other ways." He rakes his eyes over my body.

I'm curvier now than I used to be. The curves he sees now I gained from carrying our daughter. *Our daughter.* We met her father on the same day, for the first time, yet this man in front of me, he's not a stranger. I may not have the memories, but the feelings he evokes are real, and they're not just something that happens overnight. We have a past I can't remember and a future I never want to forget.

"Can you show me again?" I ask, my voice not sounding at all like my own. I wait with bated breath for his reply.

"Yeah, baby, I can show you."

"Does that mean...?" My words trail off as I let the unspoken words linger between us.

"Yes, Laney. That means I still love you. I never stopped loving you." With that, he leans in and captures my lips, and my heart.

This kiss is different than anything we've shared, at least the ones I can remember. It's more than just a firm press of his lips to mine. It's all-consuming as he traces my lips with his tongue, seeking entrance that I gladly grant him. Strong hands grip the backs of my thighs as he pulls me in closer, yet not close enough. Lifting one leg and then the other, I straddle him on the mattress. His hands move to my ass as he rocks me against him, all the while still kissing me. His mouth devours mine, and it's more than anything I've ever experienced. It's as if he's consuming me—mind, body, soul, and heart.

I rock my hips, seeking more from him. More of something I didn't realize I was missing. I don't remember sex, which means all my sexual encounters were after high school and locked away somewhere in my mind. I can't remember ever experiencing this kind of passion. My life has revolved around my daughter. I've been too afraid to venture out into the world of dating for fear of the unknown. I mean, I couldn't remember my daughter's father. My mother had me believing he was this horrible man who didn't want us. I didn't exactly have the best track record, so I steered clear. But now... now I wonder if I was subconsciously waiting for him. Waiting for my Kenton.

Kent drags his lips from mine, and I rest my forehead against his. Our chests are heaving from the exhilaration of our kiss.

"When can we tell her?"

"When do you want to tell her?"

"Now. We can leave now and go to my place. Can the two of you stay with me tonight? I need to hold you, Laney. I need my girls with me. Please." His voice is a whispered plea, and it's unnecessary. I can't explain it, but our souls are tethered together, and I want nothing more than to spend more time with him.

"Okay."

"Yeah?" He pulls back, his dark eyes filled with so much... love. Love for me and our daughter, and it's a look I never want to miss out on. Never again.

"Yes. We have to figure out where we go from here."

"You tell me, babe. I go where you go. If that's back to California, then that's where we'll be. If it's here in Tennessee, if you and Kendrix settle here in Jackson, we need to start looking for a bigger place. I want my little girl to have a nice big yard to play in."

"Um, is this yard not big enough?"

"I thought you wanted to sell this place?"

"No, that was all my mother. She insisted I sell it. She didn't want me coming here at all."

"What do you want, Delaney?"

"You and our daughter. The rest will work itself out."

"All right then, let's go get our girl. Pack a bag." He smacks me lightly on the ass, making me giggle as I climb off his lap.

Hand in hand, we go to my room, and he sits on the bed and watches me as I toss some things into an overnight bag. "I think I have what I need," I say, looking around. He doesn't speak. He grabs the bag that's still open in one hand and laces our fingers together with the other as we head to the room that Kendrix is using. I grab her what she needs, making sure I have her teddy bear, and then zip up the bag.

Without a word, he offers me his hand again, and I take it. We make our way down the steps, slowly as he's refusing to let go of me, and into the kitchen. Kendrix is sitting on the kitchen counter, with Mark standing next to her while Ridge, Seth, and Tyler are all hammering nails into what appears to be a piece of scrap wood.

"What's going on in here?" Kent asks. It's obvious to hear the joy in his voice.

"Mr. Kent, we're having a nail-hitting contest. You want to play?" Kendrix asks.

"Not right now, sweetie," I answer before he can. "How about you and I go over to Kent's house for a little while? Since our kitchen is messy, we're going to make dinner at his place."

"Yay!" she cheers. "Sketti."

"You ready, kiddo?" Kent drops my hand and walks over to her. He opens his arms and she doesn't hesitate to jump into them, letting him settle her on his hip. He smiles at her like she's the light in his life. He turns to face the guys, giving each one of them a look I can't explain, but he gets a subtle nod from all four of them.

"Ready, baby?" he asks me.

I can feel my face heat at his endearment, but I keep my head held high as I nod to him, and wave to the guys. No other words are exchanged as we load up in his truck and head toward his place.

Chapter 16

KENT

The drive to my place is quiet. Even Kendrix is not talking, and my little girl loves to talk. It's almost as if she can sense something big is about to happen. When we pull into the drive, I hustle to get her out of her seat and carry her into the house. Delaney is right behind me as she sets their bag on the floor.

"What's that, Momma?" Kendrix asks, pointing to their bag. I set her on her feet and busy myself taking her coat off her. "Can we make sketti now?" she asks me.

"In a minute, sweetie. Actually, we want to talk to you about something. Come sit down." Delaney offers Kendrix her hand, and she takes it, bouncing off to sit in the living room. Once they're settled on the couch, I take the chair sitting across the room from them. I don't know how she's going to react and I don't want to scare her. "Do you remember how Mommy told you that your daddy was away with his family?"

"Yep," my daughter replies brightly.

"Well, things have changed, and Daddy can be with us now."

"Oh." Her eyes grow wide.

"Kendrix, sweetie, Kent is your daddy." She just blurts it out like ripping off a Band-Aid. Then again, I'm not sure how else you could explain it to an almost five-year-old. We can't tell her why I was away from them, not right now. Maybe one day, when she gets older. When she can understand the depths of her grandmother's deception.

Kendrix gasps and her little hand covers her mouth. She stares at me, her big blue eyes wide and glassy with tears. "Mr. Kent?" she whispers.

"Princess, I promise you that if I could have been with you and your mommy, I would have been there. Every breath, every second, every minute, every hour of every day I would have been there."

The room is silent while we give her time to process what we're saying. I'm expecting an onslaught of questions any second now, because that's my little girl. She's curious and observant and so damn smart for her age. I watch her as she climbs down off the couch and makes her way toward me. She stops when she's standing in front of me, where I sit in the chair. She doesn't make a move to climb in my lap like she usually does so I rest my elbows on my knees, bringing myself to her level. When her tiny hands land on my cheeks and her blue eyes bore into mine, I freeze. I don't know what's happening.

"C-Can I call you daddy?" she whispers.

Her voice is so soft, I'm not even sure Delaney heard her. I get my answer when a sob rings out from across the room. It doesn't faze my daughter as she keeps her hands on my cheeks, while her momma's blue eyes remain trained on me. I open my mouth to speak, but nothing comes out. Swallowing hard, I try again. "Do you want to call me daddy?"

"I've never had a daddy," she replies while nodding.

My heart cracks wide open and allows her to reach in with her tiny little hands and burrow deep inside. "I'll always be your daddy." I want to tell her that I'm sorry, that it wasn't my fault, that nothing would have kept me away had I known, but she's a little girl who doesn't need all of that. All she needs is my reassurance that I'm her dad, and she can call me whatever in the hell she wants.

"Can we make sketti now…, Daddy?" she asks, smiling.

Elation.

Happiness.

Love.

"Yes, princess, we can make spaghetti now." She leaps into my arms, securing hers around my neck, and I hug her as tight as I can without hurting her. "Mommy," I say, finding Delaney's eyes. She's openly crying, and tears coat her cheeks, but there's a smile that greets me. It's her smile, the one I remember. I hold one hand out for her, and she comes to us. I move Kendrix to one knee and pull Delaney down onto the other. "My girls," I say, kissing Delaney.

"Ew." Kendrix giggles.

I kiss her all over her face, making her laugh even harder. "I have to pee. Mr.—Daddy, I have to pee." She laughs and I relent, letting her off my lap as she rushes down the hall.

Delaney, much like our daughter did earlier, cradles my cheeks in the palms of her hands. However, I speak before she has the chance to. "I love you." More tears well in her eyes. She doesn't say it back, and that's okay. She needs time, and I get that. I'll give her all the time she needs.

Kendrix comes racing into the room and hops back up on my lap. I have both my girls right where they belong. I feel as though it's the first time I've taken a full, even breath since the night I ghosted her. Never again. Not a day will pass that Delaney won't know what she means to me. Either of them.

An hour later, our bellies are full and my kitchen is a mess. Kendrix had a blast making spaghetti. We used box noodles and jar sauce, so I'm not sure how we were so messy, but the memory we made, that's worth all the messes.

"Kendrix."

"Daddy." She grins.

"How would you like to meet your grandma and grandpa? My mommy and daddy."

"Yay!" She cheers and I don't know if she really understands, but her enthusiasm tells me she will embrace them just as she has me. This little human is resilient and has so much love to give.

"Laney?"

"Have you told them yet?"

"No, but I was going to go call them. I thought we could swing by their place and maybe stop and get some ice cream on the way home."

"It's freezing outside."

"It's never too cold for ice cream."

"Yeah, Momma, it's never too cold," Kendrix agrees.

"I'm always going to be outnumbered with you two, aren't I?" Delaney laughs.

"Maybe the next one will be a boy and he can be on your side."

Her eyes widen before she shakes her head and smiles. "Go make your phone call, crazy man."

I toss a wink in her direction and rush to my bedroom to call my parents. I don't want to have this call in front of Kendrix.

"My son, it's been too long since I've seen you," my mom greets me.

"Hey, Mom."

"What's a mother got to do to get her only son to come and visit her?" There's humor in her voice.

"Funny you should mention that. Is Dad around?"

"He's sitting right here."

"Can you put the phone on speaker?"

"Kenton." Dad's deep baritone comes across the line.

"You're both sitting down, right?"

"We are. Are you in trouble?" my mom asks.

"No. However, I do have a story to tell you, and you're going to want to be sitting for this one."

"We're ready, son," Dad tells me.

With a deep breath in and a slow exhale, I begin the story. I start at the beginning, telling them how I met Delaney. How I kept her all for me, but there was no one I wanted more. I don't hold anything back as I spill the details of our situation.

"That poor girl," Mom comments once I'm finished.

"She's the one you used to bring to the back meadow?" Dad asks, throwing me off.

"How did you know about that?"

He chuckles. "Don't you know Dad knows everything? You'll learn with the little one of yours."

Just like that, easy and absolute acceptance of my daughter and her mother in my life. "Yes, she's the one." Those words have a double meaning. She's the girl I would bring to the meadow, but she's now the woman I plan to spend the rest of my life with.

"When do we get to meet them?" Mom inquires.

"Well, they're here with me. We just finished dinner. I thought we could stop by? Let you meet them."

"Yes," they say at the same time.

"Okay." I chuckle. "I'll load up my girls and we'll head over."

"Oh, Kenton," Mom cries.

"They're amazing, Mom." I can feel myself starting to get choked up again.

"Well, what are you doing gabbing? Hang up, get them, and bring them to me."

Dad and I both laugh this time. "We'll see you soon."

"You ladies ready to go?" I ask once I'm back in the living room.

"You tooked a long time," Kendrix says.

"I'm sorry, princess. I had to tell them all about you."

"Will they like me?"

"Come here." I lift her into my arms. "They already love you so very much. You have nothing to worry about."

"Okay, I'm ready."

"Will she always be this agreeable?" I ask Delaney. "I have a feeling we'll need to remember these days for the teenage years." This moment is surreal. I still can't believe I'm a father. That this little girl is my responsibility.

"Doubtful. She is a girl with her own mind."

"Stubborn like her momma."

"Yeah, if only I had my mind."

"Hey." I pull her in close, and now both of them are in my arms

141

where they belong. "You're still you. You might be missing a few years, but that doesn't change who you are."

"It does. You have all these memories; these moments, and I have a dream with you in it that I don't understand. You have all this… love and I feel—" She stops talking and shakes her head.

"Is that what you're worried about? That I told you I love you?"

"I-I can't say it. I don't know. There is so much going on inside of me, so many emotions."

"Laney." I lean down and kiss her temple. "There is nothing to worry about. You wanna know why?"

"Enlighten me," she says, her sadness already starting to fade.

"Because I'm going to make you fall in love with me all over again."

"You're so certain I was before? We never said it, right?"

"No, we never said it, and I'm sorry. I should have. This time, I have my second chance and I won't stop until you're head over heels in love with me."

"You seem confident."

"I am. When it comes to my girls, I am. Now, let's grab our coats and get moving. I wouldn't put it past my mother to send a search party." Delaney's eyes widen and I laugh. "She's excited to meet both of you. I think prom was the last time I took someone home."

"Prom? As in high school?"

"Yep. Now, let's get moving." I set Kendrix on her feet, and she rushes off to get her coat. I help her into it and her boots while Delaney gathers her stuff as well. I snag my jacket from the hook by the door and we're off.

Twenty minutes later, we're pulling into my parents' driveway. The front porch light, glowing bright like a beacon, calls us in. I help Kendrix out of the truck and don't even try to set her on her feet. She's a tiny thing like her momma. She might be too big for Delaney to carry her around all the time, but not for me. I intend to do it as long as she'll let me. I've missed so much with her, at least I have this.

Stepping into the house, I smell Mom's been baking, and I smile. I know as soon as the call ended, she rushed into the kitchen to make some kind of treat for my daughter. Her granddaughter. There is no doubt in my mind she's going to dote on both of my girls.

We take off our shoes and coats and follow my parents' voices to the kitchen. "Hey," I greet them.

"Oh, who do we have here?" Mom asks.

"Mom, Dad, this is Kendrix." I bounce her in my arms. "And this is Delaney." I pull her into my side with my free arm. "Ladies, these are my parents, Gordon and Georgia Baldwin."

"It's so nice to meet you." Delaney offers Mom her hand, but Mom bypasses it and pulls her into a hug. Mom pulls away and keeps her hands on Delaney's shoulders. Something passes in her expression, but it's gone before I can name it. "Welcome," Mom says softly, stepping back. I can hear the emotion in her voice. I know she's wanted me to settle down, but this is not what I expected. I knew she'd be happy and that she would love her simply because I do, but her emotions are unexpected for sure.

Delaney then turns to my dad, and he does the same. "Welcome to the family," he says softly before releasing her.

"And this little lady?" Dad steps closer and holds his arms out to Kendrix. "Come and see your papaw."

She doesn't even hesitate as she reaches for him, allowing him to take her from my arms.   "Hello, Kendrix." My mom places her hand on her arm. "I'm your mamaw."

"Hi. That's my daddy, and that's my mommy." She points to Delaney and me.

Her tiny hands squeeze my heart with her words. Such easy acceptance of me into her life. I wasn't sure how she would take it, but she's acting as if us telling her that I'm her dad is as normal as the fact that Delaney has always been her mom.

"Well, come on in and sit down. I made some cookies, but they need to cool."

"I love cookies," Kendrix tells my dad on the way to the living room.

"Yeah? What's your favorite?"

"All of them." Her tone says she's serious and it makes the four of us laugh.

Over the next hour, we sit and talk. My parents are enamored with both of them. I can see my mom's wheel spinning, and I'm sure she's wondering if and when she's going to get more grandkids.

"We should get going," I say after Kendrix yawns for the third time.

"No, I want to stay." Kendrix pouts. She's sitting on the couch between my parents and crawls up into my dad's lap. He gives us a pleading look.

"We need to get you home, kiddo."

"Hey, how about you come hang out with us this weekend? Mommy and Daddy can drop you off and we'll spend the entire day playing, and we can bake more cookies, or make a cake."

She nods then looks up at my dad. "You know how to use a hammer?"

He chuckles. "Yeah, baby girl, I can use a hammer."

"Can I?" Her big blue eyes seek out her mother and me.

I look at Delaney, waiting for her to answer, to find her watching me. "I'll let you make the call, Daddy. I don't know them, but I trust you."

"You can trust us. I promise you that. We'll take good care of her." This from my dad.

"I know that. I'm sorry… I didn't mean for it to sound like I didn't. I just… I'm not used to new people in our lives, and well, I just met you. I know that sounds crazy since we just found each other again, but I already have a deep trust with Kent. I can't explain it. I assume it's our prior connection. I just wish I could remember."

"In due time, my dear. The heart will remember in due time."

"How's Saturday afternoon?" I ask my parents.

"That's perfect."

"Great. I'll call you, but probably around one or so."

"Sounds perfect," Mom agrees.

"All right, princess, time to go." I stand, offering Delaney my hand, helping her from the couch. I then bend and take Kendrix from my dad. She comes willingly, knowing that she gets to come back. I've got this parenting thing down. After a few goodbyes, we're on our way back to my place.

"Are we sleeping here?" Kendrix asks when Delaney tells her it's time to get her jammies on.

"We are. Is that all right with you?" Delaney questions.

"Where?"

"I have a spare bedroom," I explain.

"Can I see it?"

"Sure." I hold out my hand and we walk down the hall. I stop at the spare bedroom and push open the door.

"Is this where you sleep?" She peers up at me.

"No. My room is the next one."

"Can I see that one?" she asks, bouncing on the balls of her feet.

"Of course." We take a few more steps until I'm pushing open my bedroom door. I try to look at it through their eyes. King-size bed, with a dark gray comforter tossed haphazardly over it. Two dressers and a nightstand on either side. The walls are white, as I've never taken the time to paint.

"That's a huge bed," Kendrix says, her eyes wide. "Can we sleep in here, Daddy?" The way she says daddy so easily has me agreeing before I even consult Delaney.

"You can."

"All three of us? Yay, we're having a slumber party." She turns and rushes to the living room.

"What's she doing?" I ask Delaney.

"My guess would be she's getting her jammies."

"Sorry. I couldn't tell her no."

She smiles. "You're going to have to one day, you know that, right? You're going to have to learn to tell her no."

"Really? I was hoping you could be the bad guy, and I'd be the one who makes it all better."

She throws her head back in laughter. "Not a chance, buddy. This parenting gig is hard." Her laughter fades, and her face grows serious. "It's going to be nice to have someone to share it with."

In two long strides, I'm standing in front of her. "That man is me." I bend to kiss her just as the pitter-patter of little feet comes barreling down the hall. Kendrix skids to a stop, her jammies on backward, with a book in her hand. "You ready for bed?" I ask, barely containing my laughter.

"Yep." She squeezes past our legs and tosses the book on the bed. She begins to try and climb, but the bed is too tall. "Daddy! I need help."

"I love you," I say softly to Delaney before going to rescue our daughter. "Come here, munchkin." I grab her and lightly toss her on the bed, making her giggle.

"That was fun. Do it again."

"We better not. It's time for a story and then bed."

"O-kay," she concedes and wiggles her little self under the covers right in the middle of the bed. "Come on, guys. I need my story."

I look over my shoulder at Delaney. "You heard the girl. Get moving."

"We need to change. Hold that thought, sweetie." Delaney disappears down the hall.

"I'll be right back. Can you keep the bed warm for us?" I ask, leaning over the bed, my hands pressed to the mattress.

"Yep."

"Daddy loves you, Kendrix." I'm never going to let a day go by that I don't tell them both what they mean to me.

Her eyes light up. "You love me?"

"I do, so very much."

"I love you too, Daddy, and Mommy too."

I bop her nose with my index finger. "We love you more. Be right back." I grab some pajama pants and head to the bathroom to change. It's not the night I was hoping for—holding Delaney in my arms—but it's better. I get both of my girls, and nothing is better than that.

Chapter 17

Delaney

All day long yesterday the only thing Kendrix talked about was going back to Kent's parents' house today. She asked me no less than twenty times what kind of cookies they were going to make, and if she could take her pink hammer with her. Something else, she's been thrilled about, is staying at her daddy's house. The last two nights we've stayed at his place, the three of us snuggled into his big bed. I told her no, but Kent said yes. I'm going to have to talk to him about that. She's going to expect it. She's going to get used to it, and we're never going to get her to sleep alone again.

He's spoiling her, and while I understand it, I still feel like we need to keep her grounded, as in, she doesn't get everything she wants. I know he feels guilty, but at the same time, he doesn't want to be a pushover parent. I'm going to have to broach the subject lightly. He's new to this parenting thing, and while I want him to feel comfortable, I also don't want her to be a spoiled brat.

"You ready?" Kent asks as he enters the bedroom, his bedroom.

"Yes. Where's Kendrix?"

"She's in the living room, bag in hand ready to roll." He smiles at me and it warms my heart.

"She's excited."

"She is, and what about you? Are you excited for us to spend the day together?"

"I would be more excited if you told me what we were doing."

"It's a surprise."

I shake my head and smile. I've never been one for surprises. But coming from this man, I'll take what I can get.

"I'm weady!" Kendrix yells for us.

"We better get moving."

"Kent, you know you have to stop giving in to her demands, right? And we need to make her sleep in her own bed."

"I know, but her room isn't set up here, and I need to do that. I'll get started on making her the room deserving of a princess this week."

"She doesn't need that. She just needs you to love her, spend time with her, and to know that she can't get anything she wants so easily."

"I know, but I think about all that I missed, and when she bats those long eyelashes at me, I'm toast."

"Suck it up, buttercup. Trust me, you're going to thank me in the end. She's smart, and she's already figured out that she can get her way when it comes to you. And before you say it, and if you're not going to say it, I know you're thinking it. She's going to love you no matter what. She might say otherwise in anger or trying to get her way—believe me, I've been there—but she will love you unconditionally. I promise you that."

"Just like I love her, and her momma." He bends to kiss me, and I accept his lips against mine eagerly. "Now, let's get moving, woman." He swats my ass and saunters out of the bedroom yelling out to Kendrix, letting her know the train is leaving.

Twenty minutes later, we're pulling into his parents' driveway. Knowing Kent is going to be carrying Kendrix, I reach around the seat and grab her small backpack before climbing out of the truck. I meet them in front, where he laces his hand with mine as we make our way to the front door.

"I'm hewear!" Kendrix yells as soon as we're through the front door.

"I've been waiting on you forever," Gordon says, taking her from Kent's arms.

"I know. My mommy and daddy tooked fowever."

"Took," Kent corrects her.

"There's my sweet girl." Georgia joins us. "We're getting ready to make lunch and then we'll make cookies."

"I gets to make lunch?" Kendrix asks, eyes wide.

"Of course you can."

"Yay."

"Kendrix," I say her name, and she turns to look at me. "You be good, okay?"

"I'm always good."

What can I say to that? She's right. She's such a good kid, and her sassiness has no limits. "Can Mommy have a kiss?" I step forward, and she leans out of Gordon's arms to give me a hug and a kiss on the cheek.

"Daddy too," she says, pulling away and leaning toward Kent. His dark eyes sparkle every single time she calls him daddy. I think she notices too, because she's stepped up her game. It's Daddy this and Daddy that. Then again, this is all new to her as well. I've been Mommy for almost five years. She's new to the Daddy gig, just like Kent. To see her so happy, to see them both happy warms my heart.

"Call us if you need anything," Kent tells his parents. "We're going to be around."

"What are the two of you getting into?" his mom asks. She looks at me and smiles, and it's a mix between "thank you for bringing us this precious gift of a girl," and "I have a secret." I wonder if she thinks we're going to run back to his place and hop in bed. I look at my feet to ward off the blush I feel coming on. I don't want his parents to think that of me.

He looks down at me and finds me watching him. "It's a surprise." He winks.

"Well, you kids have a good time. We've got this one." His dad smiles at Kendrix, and my heart swells at the love this family is so easily willing to give.

Don't get me wrong. My family was loving. I know they loved me, but what they did to me... I don't know that I will ever be able to forgive my parents. And my father, did he know about what she did? That's still a huge unanswered question. Did he go along with her plan? Was it his idea? Will she ever tell me? Do I really want to know?

"Laney?" I break out of my mental fog to find Kent and his parents watching me intently.

"Sorry. I was lost in thought." I offer them the brightest smile I can come up with. "Kendrix, Mommy loves you."

"I loves you too. Bye." She waves, her smile big.

"We'll be back in a few hours," Kent informs them.

"Take your time," his mom tells us again.

Hand in hand, we head back to his truck and are on our way back out of the driveway. "Where to?" I ask, hoping he's willing to give me a little bit of a hint.

"I'm taking you on a day date."

"And that would be where?" I ask again, trying to get it out of him.

"You'll see." He pulls out of the driveway and drives a few hundred feet before turning into the same road we took the day he brought us to the meadow. We bounce through the field, and the fresh layer of snow we got yesterday causes the truck to slip and slide.

"Are we going to get stuck?"

"No. I have four-wheel drive."

"Why are we sliding?"

"It's not good on ice."

"So, we're going to get stuck?"

"Relax, beautiful. We're fine." He grins over at me and quickly turns his attention back to the path in front of us. Instead of going to the open meadow, he makes a turn toward the right.

I fight the urge to ask again what we're doing, but this frustrating man next to me won't budge. Of that, I'm certain. Instead, I take in the view.

The trees are covered with snow, and they glisten and shine as the sun hits them. The sun is deceiving though. It's been well under freezing since I arrived in Jackson. It's a far cry from what I'm used to in California, but I'm enjoying the season immensely. Just another notch in the "pro" column when it comes to Tennessee.

I'm so lost in the scenery it takes me a few seconds to realize we've stopped moving. "Not to seem ungrateful, but uh, what are we doing?"

He laughs. It's a profound rumble from somewhere deep in his chest. "I'd never think that, and we're going ice skating."

"Really?" I ask, sitting up a little straighter in the seat.

"Yep. We've done this a few times, back then. When you were on winter break. This pond—can't even really be called that—is shallow. My dad dug it for my mom when they first bought the property before I was even born. She loved to ice skate. It's barely two feet deep, so it doesn't take much for it to freeze over."

"Do we have skates?"

"Yeah, we've got skates. We've also got blankets and a heavier coat and gloves for you. I even managed to sneak in some homemade hot chocolate. My mom's recipe."

"When did you manage to do all of that?"

"While you were in the shower. Kendrix was watching cartoons, and I snuck it all out to the truck."

"Is the hot chocolate still hot?"

"Yes. I have it in a Yeti bottle. It's going to be perfect. Now, you ready to do this?"

"I don't know how." I hate that insecurity washes over me. It's not only that, but I don't want to disappoint him.

"Yes, you do. I taught you. Right here in this very spot."

"Really?" There have been so many times I wished my memories from those years would appear, but never more since my time here in Tennessee. Not remembering this man is a tragedy.

He nods. "Yes, and it's just like riding a bike. It will come right back to you."

"I don't remember any of that, Kenton. You might have to teach me all over again."

151

He shrugs. "If I do, then I do. Just gives me more of a reason to hold onto you."

"Okay." I grin at him. "Let's do it."

"Be right back." After pushing open his door and getting out, he jogs around to the back of the truck. I turn in my seat and watch him out the back window as he opens the tailgate and pulls out two pairs of ice skates. He jogs to my door and I roll down the window. "Move your seat all the way back to give yourself some room, and lace up." He hands them through to me, then leans in for a kiss, before jogging back behind the truck, while I get to work putting on my skates.

"Here's the hot chocolate," he says, setting what looks like a gallon jug with Yeti spelled out on the side, and two small travel mugs that have the Beckett Construction logo on them on the center console.

I watch him move the steering wheel and begin to put his skates on. "Why don't you move your seat back?"

"Tall guy problems." He laughs. "I'm good. You ready?"

"No." I bend back over and lace up each skate. "I don't think I can walk in these."

"Sure you can, and if not, that's what I'm here for."

"What? To carry me?"

"You know it." He winks. "You good?"

"As good as I can be, I guess."

"You need another coat?"

"No, this one is warm." I dig my gloves out of my coat pocket and pull them on. I grab my hat from the dash, pull it down over my ears, and turn to look at him. "Ready." He nods, and before I can say anything else, he's out of the truck and at my door. "How did you do that so fast in these things?" He lifts me from the truck and sets me on my feet. "Wow." I wobble and hold onto him.

"I've got you. I'm not going to let you fall. Just take one small step at a time."

Slowly we make our way to the ice. "I'm not so sure about this, Kent."

He moves to stand behind me. His hands settle on my hips, and his hot breath caresses my ear. "I've got you, baby. Nothing is going to happen. If you fall, I fall, and I'm not a fan of falling."

My skin prickles from his closeness. Then again, it could be that deep timbre of his voice as he calls me baby. I never thought I'd be one for terms of endearment, but coming from Kent, they're sexy as hell.

"I've got you. We're going to put one foot in front of the other. Slow and steady."

My hands land over his where they grip my waist. "I don't know." I can hear the wobble of uncertainty in my voice.

"Trust me."

I do trust him. "Okay," I concede. Slowly, I take one small step and then another until we're standing on the ice.

"Good. Now, glide one foot forward at a time. Just small glides. I'm right here with you. I won't let you fall."

I do as he says. My legs tremble, but before I know it, we've made a full lap around the pond. "I can't believe I'm doing this."

"Want to try it on your own?"

"No."

"How about you try it holding my hand instead of me behind you?" he suggests.

"I don't know."

I feel his body move closer as his warmth seeps into my back. His lips press against my neck, and I shiver—not from being cold, but from the contact. "You can do this, Laney," he says softly.

Something flashes in my mind, and I freeze, almost causing us both to tumble to the ice.

"Laney?" he questions.

I close my eyes and try to see it. The flash. It was so quick, I don't even know what it was, but it was familiar. As if we've been in this very spot, and he's kissed my neck before.

"Delaney, are you all right? Answer me," he demands.

I turn in his arms and stare up at him. "I had a flash. I think it was a memory. We were here. I couldn't see you, but I could feel you, and you kissed my neck. I don't know for sure, but it feels like I've been here before. Like we've been here before."

"We have. And I've said those exact words to you the first time I brought you here."

"You remember that?"

"Beautiful, Laney. I remember it all. Every moment I had with you. I remember it."

"I'm jealous," I admit.

"I'll retell you every detail. In fact, I can write it down. You can read it whenever you want."

"I just want them back, Kent. I want to remember my time with you. I want to remember creating our daughter. I want to remember it all."

"I want that too, but you have to promise me something."

"Anything."

"When your memory returns and I have faith that it will, don't leave me. I was an asshole to not show up that night, and I regret it. I will always regret it. So when you remember and you're mad at me, I deserve your anger, but please don't leave me. I need you, and I need Kendrix in my life."

"We just got here," I say stupidly. His words, they make me weak in the knees, and I want to tell him that I love him too. But it's still too soon. I need more time. I feel it deep in my soul, but I need more time.

"No. You've always been here." He places our joined hands over his heart. "I just got Kendrix, but I won't let her go. I won't let either of you go."

Inch by torturous inch, his head lowers until finally, his lips press against mine. The kiss is slow as he takes his time, parting my lips and exploring my mouth. Leisurely, he kisses me as if we have all the time in the world. That's when it hits me—that we could have. I don't have to leave him or this town. My job as a graphic designer allows me to work from anywhere, and with my inheritance, I don't have to worry about a salary that will support me and Kendrix. We're covered.

"I could kiss you for hours," Kent says breathily against my lips.

"Yeah? Maybe we should go somewhere a little warmer and test that theory."

"Don't tease me, woman." He kisses me one more time then pulls away. "You ready to go?"

"Will there be more kissing?"

"That wasn't in the plan, but we can make that happen. Nothing is set in stone for today. I just wanted to spend some time with you, and I thought maybe, just maybe doing something that we used to do, might jog your memory."

"I think it worked. I don't really know, but the moment was oddly familiar as it played out in my head."

"Good."

"Hot chocolate and back to your place?"

"As you wish." He helps me off the ice, then carries me to the truck. Pulling the keys out of his pocket, he hits the remote start then opens the door, and sets me on the seat, helping me out of my skates. "Hand me my boots, will you?"

I hand them over. He kisses me, grabs my skates, and shuts me in the cab of the truck. I hear the tailgate lower, and I know he's taking his skates off and putting his boots back on outside. He's so tall I'm surprised he was able to get them on in here. A few minutes later, he's back in the truck, and I hand him the hot chocolate I poured for him.

"Thanks, babe."

I watch as he chugs the hot liquid. He's even sexy when he drinks. I'm not sure what this man is doing to me, but he has me doing and thinking things that are out of my comfort zone. Although, from what he tells me, it didn't used to be. I want so badly to get back there. I know he wants it too, but he's worried. If what he tells me is true, if my memories ever come back and they match up to what he's told me, I forgive him. How could I not? He's shown me over and over again how sorry he is and that he's changed. People make mistakes, and I, for one, am not going to make the mistake that I feel would be the biggest of my life.

Leaving him again.

I won't do it.

Chapter 18

KENT

I had planned to take her to an early dinner, but bringing her back to my place—at her request to see if I can live up to the challenge of kissing her for hours—is a plan I can get on board with. It's not like it's something we haven't done before. There were times when I would keep my lips fused with hers for hours on end. Never taking it further, just enjoying her taste and the feel of her in my arms. I didn't want to tell her that though. She remembered a little today at the pond, or really, it's just a huge water hole, but it's all the same. I don't want to tell her this time. I want to see if she remembers anything on her own.

"I'm going to call Mom and Dad and check on our girl." I push open the front door and allow her to walk in before me.

"Good idea."

We kick off our shoes and strip out of our coats before getting comfortable on the couch. Pulling my phone out of my pocket, I dial Dad's number, but he doesn't answer. I then dial Mom, and she answers right away.

"Hello," she whispers.

"Mom, why are you whispering? What's going on?" I can feel panic start to rise that something might be going on with my daughter.

"Because your father and our granddaughter are sleeping next to me."

My shoulders relax. I look over at Delaney and smile, letting her know everything is okay. I know she could hear the worry in my voice, and I refused to look at her as I questioned my mother. "Has she been good? Is she okay? Asking for us?" I fire off questions.

"She's an angel, Kenton. She's so precious and she's not asked for you once." She chuckles. "I know as a parent that hits the heartstrings, but that's a good thing. She feels safe and comfortable with us, as she should."

"No, I agree with you. I'm glad she's having a good time. I can't believe you got her to nap. She doesn't do that for us." I look at Delaney and she nods her agreement.

"Well, I guess it's cuddles with Papaw that do the trick. I'll send you a picture. How's your day?"

"Going great. We went skating at the pond, and we just got back home to… warm up a little."

"Well, you kids have a good day. Don't rush back. We're enjoying our time with her. I think I might take me a little nap with them."

"Thanks, Mom. Love you."

"I love you too, son."

I end the call and fill Delaney in on our conversation just as my phone pings with a message. I pull it up and see a picture of my dad asleep on the couch, with Kendrix curled up in his lap. He has his arms around her holding her to him even in his sleep.

"They're so good with her. She must be at ease to take a nap."

"Yes. And even though I know they're great, I mean they raised me, it's still nice to see her so relaxed. Now we can enjoy the rest of our day."

"Kissing."

"Trust me, I didn't forget." Leaning into her, I slide my hand behind her neck and pull her into me. "I never thought I'd get the chance to be with you here, like this again. Now that I am, I never want to let you go."

"Then don't," she whispers. Her voice is thick, and when her tongue darts out to lick her lips, I'm done talking.

My lips seek hers and I waste no time pushing past them, having her open for me. Her taste explodes on my tongue as I explore her mouth. Every touch we've ever shared, every kiss of hers I've tasted, it all comes rushing back to me, as if no time had passed. No one has ever affected me the way she does.

My lips trail down her neck, and I want to strip her bare and worship her body. I want to remind her with my mouth, my hands, and my cock how explosive we can be. Reining it in, I move back to her mouth, kissing her like my life depends on it.

When she pushes against my chest, I feel my shoulders drop. This is too much for her. No matter how badly I want it, want her, I need to give her time. I'm a stranger to her, essentially. So, when she climbs on my lap to straddle me, I'm shocked. My hands grip her ass as I lift my hips, pushing my hard cock into her core.

"Oh," she breathes.

Loving her reaction, I do it again. This time, I pull her toward me, rocking her body over my erection while thrusting my hips, and she moans. It's a low, deep, sexy sound from somewhere in the back of her throat. The sound goes straight to my cock as I thicken, something I didn't think was possible. The pain from the zipper in my jeans is more uncomfortable than anything, but I refuse to stop. No way in hell am I stopping this. I can deal.

With my hands on her ass and my lips suckling her neck, she takes the lead and rocks her hips, seeking her release that I am all too willing to give her. Her breathing is accelerated, and her movements grow faster until they stop altogether.

"Laney?" I ask when she buries her face in my neck. "Look at me."

She shakes her head and mumbles, "No."

"Come on, beautiful, let me see those eyes." It takes her a few moments, but she eventually sits up and looks at me. Her cheeks are pink, and she's biting down on her bottom lip. "Talk to me. What just happened?"

"It's embarrassing."

159

"There is nothing you can't tell me, Laney. Nothing. What's going on in the gorgeous head of yours?"

"I—" She stops and closes her eyes. I watch as she slowly inhales and exhales, squaring her shoulders as her eyes slide open. "I don't remember sex. I mean, I know what it is, I remember that, but I don't remember the act."

"You might not, but I do." I hate we're about to have this conversation, but she needs it. "We talked about everything. You want me to tell you?"

"That's so wrong," she says. "I can't expect you to do that. Talk about me with other people."

"Trust me, it's not a picnic, but I'll do it for you. I have your memories, and like I said earlier, I'll give them to you. As little or as much as you want."

She nods. "I-I assume I wasn't sexually active until college since I have no memory of ever actually, you know." She shrugs.

"Your freshman year." I stop, preparing myself to tell the woman I love about her sexual experience with a man who's not me. "He pursued you for a couple of weeks, and you met up with him at a frat party. You said he was sweet and gentle, and told you he cared about you." I have to focus to not let my anger at how he treated her show through. I have to deliver the information. "You went up to his room. You said he was easy with you, but it was all about him. You didn't come." Her cheeks glow crimson. "Fifteen minutes later, he climbed out of bed and got dressed. I'm paraphrasing when I tell you that he said something along the lines of it's been fun, you can show yourself out. You got dressed, held your head high, and left the party. You went home and cried for the rest of the weekend. Two months later, you were home on Summer break, and we met. I took you back to my place, and you were worried I'd never want to see you again. I assured you that I would. You kept telling me that it was okay, you knew the score this time and you were good with it. The next morning, you tried to sneak out of my bed, but I wouldn't let you. We spent two days holed up here." I look around. "I can see you here. It's part of why I'm still here. Part of me didn't want to give up those memories, and the other part was hoping one day you'd show up on my doorstep."

"Instead, you showed up on mine."

"Yeah." I brush a strand of hair out of her eyes.

"So, just him and you?"

I nod. "There was no one else after our first weekend together. Every time you came home, we were together. We never labeled us, and I regret that as much as I do standing you up that night. Well, I showed up, just too late."

"I don't remember, yet being here with you, it feels familiar. I can't explain it. I feel safe with you. Comfortable."

"You are safe with me," I assure her. "Never be afraid to tell me what you want, what you like, what you don't like. Not just with sex, with everything in life. I want to be your partner, Laney. Nothing you ever tell me would change that."

She nods, and a slow, shy smile tilts her lips. "Did we—" She pauses as if collecting her thoughts. "Did we make love? Or you know, did we just have sex?"

"Both. There were some days we wanted it slow, and others fast and dirty." My cock twitches, and from the way her eyes widen, she feels it.

"Show me."

"Which one?" I keep my eyes trained on her, and focus on deep, even breaths. My cock twitches, more than ready to show her everything. However, I need her to make this call. I need her to tell me exactly what she wants. I want her to be in control. I also need her to know she's safe with me.

"All of it."

"My pleasure." Pushing to my feet with her in my arms, I carry her down the hall to my bed. I don't stop until she's lying back on the bed, with me between her legs. "Tell me what you want first. This is your show, Laney."

"I-I don't know."

"Yes, you do. Tell me what you want."

"I want the ache to go away."

I kiss her neck as I grind my hips into her center. "Here?" I whisper next to her ear.

"Y-Yes." She swallows hard.

Standing tall, my hands go to her waist, and I slide my hands into the waistband of her yoga pants. With a tug, I begin stripping her bare. "Lift for me." She does as I ask and with a yank, her panties and pants are tossed to the side. Dropping to my knees, my lips press to her inner thighs.

"Kenton," she breathes. I look up to find her lifted up on her elbows watching me. "What are you doing?"

"I'm going to take the ache away."

"Oh."

Her mouth forms the cutest O, and I can't help but remember what it felt like when she would take my cock in her mouth. I was her first, something I was damn proud of. Shaking out of the memory, I get back to business. With my index fingers, I trace her folds, and she's already wet for me.

"Oh, God."

I smile. It's time to give my girl what she wants. I run my fingers through her folds one last time, pushing one inside her. Her hips lift off the bed, and her need fuels me. Lowering my head, I flatten my tongue and swipe across her clit, causing her hands to grip my hair and her legs to tighten around my shoulders. Perfect. A few more gentle caresses of my tongue and I'm adding another digit, but I'm done teasing her. I need her to come, and I desperately need to be inside her. I suck on her clit while pumping my fingers in and out of her. Her legs shake, and I'm sure I'll have a bald spot from the grip she has on my hair, but I don't relent. I take what I want, and give her what she needs at the same time.

"I-I can't... oh, God." She's incoherent, unable to form sentences. I suck harder. "Kenton!" She cries out for me as her body squeezes my fingers as her release coats my face and hands.

Fuck, I've missed her.

I kiss her everywhere my mouth will reach and don't remove my hand from between her legs until the final ripples of pleasure have left her body. Sitting back on my heels, I wipe my face with the back of my hand and stand. Her cheeks are flushed, a thin sheen of sweat on her forehead, and her eyes are hooded. She's sated and fucking more beautiful than I've ever seen her.

"Now what?" she asks once she's caught her breath and sees me watching her.

"You tell me what you want." I reach down and adjust my cock that is painfully hard.

"You."

"You have all of me."

"I wasn't finished." She smiles a lazy, sated smile. "I want you inside me."

"Strip." My voice is deep and controlled, leaving no room for negotiation. I need her naked, all of her. Her shirt and bra need to go. She holds her hand out to me and I help her sit up, then quickly take a step back. Pulling my shirt over my head, I drop it to the floor, before popping the button on my jeans and pulling them along with my boxer briefs off at the same time. My hard cock salutes her as she reaches behind her and unsnaps her bra. She lays it on her shirt beside her on the bed. Grabbing them, I toss them to the floor.

"Lie back on the bed." I reach to the nightstand and grab a condom, and within seconds, I'm sheathed and ready to devour her. Placing my knees on the bed, I crawl to her and settle between her thighs.

"This is my first time. I mean, not really, but… I'm nervous."

"Don't be nervous. If you want me to stop, just tell me. There are no expectations here."

"What if I'm bad at it?"

"You're not." I tap the side of my head, letting her know I remember.

"That was the old me. What if the new me isn't?"

"You're still you, Laney. You're the same vibrant, gorgeous, loving girl who stole my heart all those years ago. You might be missing a few of the pieces of what made you that way, but you're still you. My heart still beats for you."

"Have you always been a sweet talker?"

I chuckle. "Only with you."

"Slow. I think I'd like you slow."

"Anything you want, beautiful." Resting my weight on my elbows on either side of her head, I push her hair out of her eyes. "If at any time you want me to stop, just say the word." She nods. I align my cock with her pussy and push in—slowly, an inch at a time, giving her time to get used to my size. "It's been too long," I whisper. My lips find hers and I get lost in her.

"More," she mumbles against my lips. "I need more."

I push in further and bite down on my cheek. She feels too fucking good. "I missed you."

"There was really no one else?"

"No. I tried a few times. I'm not going to lie. I wanted to get over you. I foolishly thought that would help, but I could never go through with it. Not when you were all I could see."

She moves her hand to rest over my heart. "You have a great big heart in that chest of yours, Kenton Baldwin."

"It's tied up," I confess. "There's this girl, blonde hair, big blue eyes, and a body that could bring a man to his knees. She got her hooks in me a few years ago, and never let go, and now—" I kiss her because I want to and because I can. "There's this other girl, cute as hell, big blue eyes like her momma, and dark hair like her daddy. Like me. She's following in her momma's footsteps."

Her eyes well with tears. "I'm so happy we found you."

"Me too, baby." I slide all the way in, and my eyes roll back in my head. My head falls and I bury it in her neck, breathing her in. I relish the feel of her body surrounding mine, her warmth, and her embrace.

Her arms wrap around my shoulders, hugging me tightly. "Are you okay?" she murmurs.

"I'm just memorizing this moment. I never thought I'd be here again with you, and now that I am, I'm taking the time to savor it. To savor you. I didn't do that enough before. We were always sneaking in time before your parents needed you home. Your mom kept you busy to keep you away from me."

Her legs lock behind my ass, and her arms tighten around my shoulders. "Make love to me, Kenton."

So I do.

Slowly, I glide in and out—over and over again, all while staring into her eyes. The connection we share is deep. It's rooted in our souls, and I know her body remembers as she takes me inside her. Her mind might not know me, but her body does. We're in perfect sync. With every thrust, every touch, every kiss, we come together like a beautiful song.

Time passes by as we get lost in each other.

Kiss after kiss.

Touch after touch.

I can't get enough of her. I never want this moment to end. "Never again, Laney. I can never lose you again."

"Never." Her body tightens around me. She calls out my name, and I'm done. I can't hold on any longer as I spill over inside her, filling the condom that separates us.

My forehead rests against hers until I can catch my breath. I then slowly ease myself from her body and climb out of bed. I rush toward the bathroom, toss the condom in the trash, and grab a washcloth to clean us up with. I know it's not her first time, but in a way, it is, and I need to show her what she means to me by taking care of her. It's my job to take care of her, and I will forever and always.

After cleaning us both up, I toss the washcloth into the hamper and crawl back into bed. I open my arms for her and she comes willingly, resting her head on my chest. My hand traces her spine as we enjoy this moment.

"What are you thinking about?"

"You. Us. Kendrix. I meant what I said, Laney. I never want to be away from either of you ever again. So, you need to tell me what we're going to do."

"What do you mean?"

Here goes nothing.

I'm putting it all out there on the line. No holding back. "Where do you want to live, Laney? Here or California?"

"This is your home."

"And California is yours."

She's quiet, and I don't push her for more. I know she's processing something; she used to do it then as well. She's still my Laney—just forgetful. "California has never felt like home as much as Tennessee has since I've been here."

"I go where you go. You and Kendrix, that's what I need to make my life complete, and you know, maybe a brother or sister, possibly both, for Kendrix." There's hope in my voice, and it's real. I would love to have more babies with her. To get to experience it every step of the way.

To watch her body grow and change with our baby. I never thought of pregnancy as sexy until I pictured Laney pregnant with our baby.

"What does that mean? For us, I mean?"

I roll out from under her so we're both lying on our sides. I need her to see me face-to-face when I say this. "To me, that means that you are the love of my life, and I want to spend the rest of my life loving you. That means I want you and Kendrix to have my last name. That means that nothing and no one will ever keep you from me again."

"What if I told you I didn't want us to be together? What then?"

My heart stalls in my chest. It's not really an option for me, but I have to consider that's what could happen. "I'd never stop trying to make you fall in love with me. However, if that were the case, I'd still follow you wherever you go. Our little girl deserves both of us in her life. I won't settle for anything less for her."

Her eyes well with tears. "Can I tell you a secret?" she asks softly.

"You can tell me anything."

"I could fall in love with you."

My heart that was just stalled kicks into overdrive, and I feel as though it could beat right out of my chest. I know it's not a confession, but it's the next best thing in our situation. "Can I tell you a secret?" I ask once I can breathe right again.

"Anything."

"I won't stop until you do."

The smile that crosses her face is pure joy. Not just an "I'm happy to be here or good to see you" smile. It lights up her face. Her blue eyes sparkle, and I feel her happiness in my soul.

"We should probably go get our girl."

It's the first time she's referred to her as ours, and it sounds like she means it. "Shower, then Kendrix. Why don't we swing by the house and get some more of your stuff? I want you all to stay with me. There's no point in living in a construction zone. You can hang out here during the day, or stop by the house, whatever works, but I want you both with me."

"Okay."

"Just like that?"

"Just like that. How else are you supposed to have a chance to make me fall in love with you?"

"Good point." I kiss her hard and climb out of bed, offering her my hand. With her hand in mine, I lead her to the bathroom. Once the water is hot, we step under the spray, and her soft hands begin to roam over my body. A man can only take so much. Climbing out of the shower, dripping water all over the floor, I rustle around in the drawers for a condom. Ripping it open, I cover my hard cock and step back in the shower. Without warning, I lift her in my arms. She yelps in surprise but wraps her body around mine. Pushing her back against the wall, I slide home and fuck her against the shower wall. It's fast and dirty and even though it's a complete contrast to earlier in my bed, it's no less intimate.

It's us, and it's perfect.

Chapter 19

Delaney

Today has been perfect. I've never felt this undeniable happiness than when I'm with Kent. Something told me that I needed to come here. That it needed to be me who oversaw the renovations of the house, but never in my wildest dreams did I imagine how much it would change my life. The odds of us finding our way back to each other, without my memory, was slim, but fate was on our side.

Not just fate, but my father. He left the house to me. He wanted me to come back here. It's almost as if he knew that I would defy my mother and visit the estate before selling it. In fact, I would bet he knew the thought of selling it hurt my heart. Almost as much as me not being able to remember it.

My phone rings, pulling me out of my thoughts, and I dig it out of my purse. "Hello."

"Ms. Nottingham, Harold Garcia. How are you?"

"Hi, Mr. Garcia. I'm doing well. The remodel is moving along smoothly."

"That's why I was calling. I have something for you. It was in your father's will that I not give it to you until you'd had experienced Tennessee for yourself. I just got a call from your mother, and the conversation led me to believe that you have indeed experienced our great state."

"I have, in a sense, but it's more the people." I glance over at Kent, and he smiles from his seat behind the wheel of his truck. "We're actually on our way to the estate now. Do you need to meet up with me today?" I find it odd he's calling on a Saturday afternoon. Whatever my mother said to him must have him feeling as though he needs to act promptly.

"I can meet you there. An hour?"

"Sure. We're on our way there now. We'll wait for you."

"See you soon." He ends the call.

"That's weird." I explain the conversation to Kent.

"Something from your dad's will? Maybe it's the deed?"

"No. I already have the deed. Much to my mother's dismay. Apparently, she called him. I didn't ask him what she wanted. Looks like we're going to find out soon enough. Should we call your parents? Check on Kendrix?"

"Nah, she's fine… unless you want to?"

"Do you mind?"

"Of course not. Here." He pulls his phone out of his pocket and hands it to me, rattling off the access code.

"Just like that?"

"Just like what?"

"You give me your code?"

"Laney, you own me, heart and soul. The password to my cell phone is nothing compared to what I've already given you." Reaching over, he rests his hand on my thigh.

Unlocking the screen, I scroll through his recent calls. "Should I call your mom or your dad?"

"Either."

Knowing he called his mom earlier, I hit her contact and place the phone to my ear. It rings twice before she answers.

"Hello."

"Hi, Georgia, it's Delaney."

"Oh, hi, sweetheart."

"How's Kendrix?"

"She's perfect. We just built a fort in the living room."

"I bet she loves that."

"She's having a ball. We are too. She's something else."

"Thank you for watching her. Can I speak to her?"

"Oh, don't thank us for watching our granddaughter. That's an honor. Just a sec."

I hear her call out to Kendrix, and then her little feet and her voice as she grows closer. "Hi, Mommy."

"Hi, sweetie. Are you having a good time?"

"Yes." She rattles on about cookies, and movies, and forts and popcorn and if it were possible, my heart would be smiling. I love seeing her so excited. My mom never plays with her, and my dad, well, he was too busy working all the time. She's loving the attention, love, and affection they are showering her with.

"Daddy and I are going to go to the big house and grab some clothes. We're going to stay at his house again tonight."

"I wanna stay here and sleep in my fort."

"You do?"

"Yep."

"Okay, let me talk to Daddy, and we can decide when we get there."

"Okay, Mommy, bye. Love you. Mamaw hewear." The phone clatters to the table, causing me to pull it away from my ear, and then Georgia is back on the line.

"Sorry about that. You kids take your time. We're enjoying our day."

"Thank you. We're going to run by my house. We have a few things to pick up, and then we'll be there to get her."

"She's welcome to spend the night."

"Okay. I'll talk to Kent. Either way, we'll be there."

"Sounds good, sweetheart. Talk to you soon," she says, and the line goes dead.

"She having fun?" Kent asks.

"Yes. Apparently, they built a fort."

He nods. "Yeah, we used to do that all the time when I was a kid."

"She wants to spend the night."

"How do you feel about that?"

"I don't know. She's only ever stayed with my mom without me, and that was just recently when I came here."

"Don't worry about offending them. You decide what you feel is best for you and Kendrix."

"And you?"

"I'm going with whatever makes you the most comfortable. Baby steps and all that."

"We're hardly taking baby steps."

"Not us, Laney. I meant you and Kendrix with my parents. There are no baby steps where we're concerned. It's more of a sprint. No steps." He laughs.

"Who's that?" I ask, my attention pulled from our conversation to the car sitting in front of my house.

Kent stops the truck, and the front door of the house opens, and low and behold, there stands my mother. "Shit," Kent mumbles.

"What is she doing here?"

"Only one way to find out." He reaches for his door, but my hand on his arm stops him.

"You don't have to deal with her. I know you said she treated you badly in the past. I don't want you to have to deal with that."

"Laney, we're a team, and I can handle anything she throws my way. I have my girls, and that's what matters to me. She can spew her hatred for me. Besides, she's the one who lied to you. My guess is she's here to grovel."

"You don't know my mother."

"Then she's trespassing. We call the cops if she refuses to give us the key that she obviously has, and leave."

"This is going to get ugly."

"She brought this on herself, Delaney. Not you. You are innocent in all of this."

I nod. I know he's right, but I just don't want to deal with her. Today has been amazing, one of the best I can ever remember, and now she's here to ruin it. With a heavy sigh, I reach for the handle and climb out of his truck. Kent is waiting for me, his hand stretched out for mine, and I don't hesitate to take it. Hand in hand, we make our way onto the porch to face my mother.

"Well, don't the two of you look cozy," she sneers.

"What are you doing here, Mother?"

"This is my house."

"No, it's not. This is my house. I have the deed in my name. Dad left it to me."

She mumbles something under her breath about how she can't believe he did that. "Semantics. I'm contacting an attorney. This place should have been mine. You are my daughter, I fought for you, and you will listen to me."

"What are you doing here?" I ask her again. She's lost her damn mind. What does she mean she fought for me? I've never seen her fight for anything in her entire life. She manipulates and bosses, never fights.

"I never left. I've been staying in town. I wanted to give you a few days to cool down and come to your senses, but now I see I was wrong in doing that. You let this man get his hooks in you. You always were so naïve, Delaney. You can't believe everything you're told."

"That's rich coming from you. You mean the way I believed my mother when she told me the father of my child didn't want us?" Kent squeezes my hand. I know my words affect him, but he's letting me fight this battle on my own. His silent support means everything to me.

"I did what was best for you. Look at him, Delaney. He's trash. You deserve better."

"Trash? Are you kidding me right now? He's the best person I know. And you're right. I do deserve better. Better than a mother who would lie to me, better than a mother who has manipulated me and taken advantage of my lost memory to mold my life the way you saw fit. You robbed us of time. You robbed Kendrix of her father. You're the trash, Mother."

"Where is my granddaughter?"

"With her grandparents."

"What?" she screeches. "You left her with his family? You don't even know them. You're unfit. I didn't want to have to do this, but you aren't capable of raising her."

"The hell I'm not!" I scream. I drop Kent's hand and take the three remaining steps so we're face-to-face. "She's my daughter. I have raised her on my own!" I scream, not giving a shit who hears me. "She doesn't know her father because of you. Your lies. He's a good man, and they're good people. She's happy, healthy, and safe." I shake my head, barely controlling my rage. "You're not welcome here, Mother. Leave."

"No. I have every right to be here."

Before I can answer her, a black sedan pulls into the driveway, and Mr. Garcia climbs out. Kent looks at me and motions with his head as he turns to walk back down the steps to greet him. I'm sure he's trying to prevent him from hearing the argument.

"Look at you. Following him like some lovesick fool. If you continue to see him, I will take you to court. I will take her from you."

"Excuse me? Do you actually think a judge is going to take a little girl from her parents? We are her parents, not you. You have no case."

"You're unfit, leaving her with strangers."

I can't help it. I laugh. Not just a "ha ha" laugh, but a deep "throw your head back, deep in your gut" laugh. She's delusional, and I hate I'm just now seeing this side of her. She manipulated me for years, and now she's not getting her way, her true colors come out. I remember her being controlling growing up, but I chalked that up to my being a teenager and rebelling. But this, this is another level, and I can't help but wonder how many fights like this we had about Kenton.

"You've lost your damn mind. Go home, Mother. You're not welcome here."

"No, I'm not leaving without my granddaughter. If you want to slum it, that's fine, but you won't subject her to that."

"He's her father!" I roar. I take a step toward her. "You have no rights to our daughter. None. The game is over. You lost. Move on." I turn on my heel. I can't look at her, and there is no reasoning with her. She's lost her mind.

"Delaney!" she screams, and I ignore her until I feel a yank at my hair. The pain is instant, and so is what happens next. I feel my feet slip out from under me, the thin layer of snow frozen over has me slipping. I hear Kenton call out for me. I feel the pain as it radiates in my hip as I go down and then nothing. My world fades to dark.

Beep. Beep. Beep.

The annoying sound pulls me from sleep. Slowly, I force my eyes open and am greeted with soft white lights. Turning my head, I see Kent sitting in a chair. His head is resting on the side of the bed, my hand held tight in his. I take a minute to survey what I'm feeling. My hip hurts, my wrist is wrapped, and other than that, I feel fine. I woke up initially in the ambulance on the way to the ER. Kent was there, by my side, like a pillar of strength.

How could my mother say such awful things about a man like him? He's selfless and loving, and it's his honesty that's helped me see what was really happening. My mother spent years manipulating me. I feel like such a fool. While I know it's the memory loss, I hate that I couldn't see through her and her lies.

Looking at him sleeping at my bedside, my heart is full. He's everything I never knew I really wanted. Then again, I guess I did know back then. I like the thought of even then, I knew he was special.

"Kent," I whisper, wiggling my fingers, trying to get his attention.

His head pops up and his eyes are red. "Laney," he exhales.

"How long have I been here?"

"Just a few hours."

"Kendrix?"

"She's with my parents. I told them not to tell her. I called her and told her she got to have a sleepover. She was excited. When she asked to talk to you, I told her you were sleeping, and that you loved her." His voice cracks.

"My mother?"

"The waiting room. I told them she wasn't allowed back. She fought it until Mr. Garcia and I told them how you fell. She's lucky they don't haul her ass off to jail."

"It wasn't an accident. I don't think she meant to hurt me, but she meant to grab for me."

"I know. Fuck, Laney, you could have been hurt so much worse. You need to decide if you want to press charges."

"No. I just want it to be over. I know she's beating herself up about this. She's controlling but she's not violent. This has never happened before. She felt like she was losing control. She lost control." I pause, trying to take stock of my injuries. "What's the verdict?"

"Bruised hip, sprained wrist. You'll be sore for a few days, but you're going to be fine." He stands and kisses my cheek before burying his face in my neck. "I missed you, Laney," he whispers, and something flashes in my mind. It's the two of us lying in… a bed? He whispers those same words to me. It's the same deep timbre of his voice and the warmth his words cause inside.

"Kent."

"Yeah, baby?" He pulls back, and his red-rimmed eyes find mine.

"Have you said that to me before? That you missed me?"

"Of course I have. I always missed you when you went back to school."

"I-I remember us lying in a bed and you saying that to me."

He smiles. "Every damn time. Every time you came home, I told you that. You remember?"

"It's more of a flash, a snippet in time, but I remember, or at least I think I do. It's too much like déjà vu for it not to be real."

"It's real."

I smile. It's such a small thing, but it gives me hope that I'll remember it all one day. I want our time together. "How long do I have to stay?"

"Knock, knock," a male voice says, entering the room. "I'm Dr. Whitman. You took a nasty tumble," he tells me.

"Ice-covered stairs."

He chuckles. "You're not the first and certainly won't be the last." He goes on to tell me about my bruised hip and sprained wrist. "You need to take it easy for a few days and let your body heal. I'll send the nurse in with discharge papers."

"Dr. Whitman, I was in an accident and lost my memory from a small period of time. Could this fall, could that make my memories come back?"

He smiles sadly. "No. However, that doesn't mean they won't. The brain can be confusing, but often we find those memories are blocked due to trauma or some other contributing factor. It's a coping mechanism."

"What if someone told you lies about that time in your life? All of my memories are back except for the timeframe I was lied to."

He nods. "It's possible."

"I remembered something today, just before you came into the room. So, it's not correlated to the accident?"

"I'm sorry, but no. However, whatever you're doing to trigger those memories, keep it up. Are they good memories?"

I glance over at Kent. "The best."

"Good, then I would encourage you to stay on the course and don't try so hard. One day you might just wake up and remember it all. There is also the chance that you will never get those memories back. Like I said, the brain can be confusing."

"Thank you, Doctor."

"Sure. Anymore questions?"

"No."

"All right, I'll send the nurse in and we'll get you out of here."

Before the door is completely closed, Kent is leaning over me in the hospital bed. "I love you."

I want to tell him I love him too, but I can't. I feel this deep connection to him, but I can't seem to let myself give in to it. I wish I could remember our past so we could so easily move into our future.

"Can we go get Kendrix when we get out of here?"

"It's late, babe. Let's call and see if she's sleeping. If so, we'll get her first thing in the morning. I promise."

"Okay."

He pulls out his phone and dials his mom, putting the call on speaker so I can hear her.

"How is she?" is her greeting.

"She's going to be just fine. How's my princess?" he asks.

"Asleep in the fort. Poor thing was tuckered out. Even with her nap. We were waiting on your call before we went to bed ourselves."

"Laney is going to be fine. Thank you for watching her. I'll be by to get her in the morning."

"Why don't we bring her to you? I'll bring breakfast."

"You don't have a car seat."

"We do, actually. Ridge brought us one of theirs just in case we needed to leave."

I watch as he swallows. "Okay." He clears his throat. "That works for us. Thank you."

"You're welcome. Take care of Delaney. We've got Little Miss taken care of."

"Thanks, Mom, love you."

"Love you too. Give Delaney our best."

"Will do." He ends the call and slides the phone back in his pocket. "All is good."

"Your friends and family, they're amazing."

"Yes, they are."

"You can't leave that. The support that they give you is… it's unheard of. You can't leave that. You can't leave them."

"What I can't do is live hundreds of miles away from you. That's what I can't do."

"You won't have to."

"No?"

I shake my head. "We're staying here. I can work anywhere, and I don't want her to miss out on this. All the family and friends. We don't have this back in California."

"What about your mom?"

"She has some big changes to make if she wants to be in our lives. I won't tolerate her outburst today, and never in front of Kendrix. You're in our lives to stay."

"Yeah?" He grins.

"As just the father of your child?"

"No. You're more than that. I need some time to work it all out in my head. I'm scared, but I know you're more than just her father. You mean something to me."

"I'm not going anywhere, Laney. You take all the time that you need."

Chapter 20

KENT

I wake to the sun streaming through the blinds, and I shut my eyes to ward off the rays. Rolling over, I smile when I see Delaney sleeping peacefully. Her body is sore from the fall. No matter how many times she begged me to hold her last night, I was afraid I would hurt her. I settled for lying next to her, my head resting on her chest. Her hands stroking my hair. Neither of us said much, and that's okay. She's here, she's healthy, and she's not leaving. That's what matters.

I watch her as time passes us by. Mom texted me last night and told me to send her a message when we were up and moving today. She didn't want to keep Delaney from resting. So I'm not worried about visitors, at least not this early. When her eyes flutter open and those baby blues land on me, she smiles. Her smile lights up my entire fucking world.

"Morning, beautiful."

"Good morning."

"How you feeling?"

"Stiff."

"Let me get you some medicine." Tossing the covers off, I head to the kitchen to get her a glass of water and some over-the-counter pain reliever. I rush back to the bedroom, help her sit up, at which she rolls those baby blues, and then hand her the water and pain reliever.

"I'm not broken, Kent."

"I know you're not broken, but I'm here so I can help you. It won't be that way tomorrow when I go back to work."

"Kendrix will be here. She likes to help."

"She's going to love that."

She chuckles. "Yes, she is." She hands me the glass and I set it on the nightstand. "What time is it?"

"Just after seven."

"What time are they coming?"

"I told Mom I would text her."

"I should get up and get moving so they can come over."

"There's no rush."

"I don't want your parents to have to watch her again today."

"Delaney." I reach out and cradle her face in the palm of my hand. "Baby, it's fine. I promise. They would keep her forever if we let them. She's not a burden to them. I can guarantee you they're enjoying their time with her as much as she is with them. They've been waiting for me to settle down and give them grandkids. She's being spoiled rotten. That you can count on."

"I know they're taking good care of her, but I don't want to use them like that."

"Like what? Like two loving grandparents who are enjoying the hell out of getting to know their only granddaughter. Trust me, they want us to use them. Just wait and see. They'll be calling and asking to keep her all the time."

"Really?"

"Yes. Why are you so surprised?"

"That's not what I'm used to. My mother would complain if I asked her to watch Kendrix for me. Didn't matter that it was usually for school or for work. She would complain. My dad, on the other hand, if he was home, he was glad to watch her, but he never did fun things like build a fort in the living room with her. It's just… different and amazing. I don't want her to lose that."

"She won't lose it. They're her family."

She nods. "So are we staying in bed or are we getting ready?"

"I'd love to choose option number one, but I can see in your eyes that you need a hug from our little girl."

"I miss her."

"Come on then. Up you go." I stand to help her from the bed. I walk her to the shower, turning on the hot spray, and then help her remove her clothes. There's no messing around, just a few kisses as she lets me wash her body. No way am I going to risk hurting her. I know she's just bruised, but she's still hurt, and I won't risk that. Not with her.

Once we're out of the shower and I get Delaney propped up on the couch—though not without her complaints that she's fine—I call my parents. "They're on their way," I tell her. "Mom made a casserole or something so it's ready to eat."

"They didn't have to make breakfast."

I shrug. "That's just Mom. That's what she does. I'm going to call Ridge and thank him for the car seat." I tap his contact in my phone, and on the fourth ring, he finally answers.

"Hello."

"Knox?"

"Yep. Do you want my daddy?"

"I do, is he there?"

"Yep. My mommy is froing up so I'm watching my sister."

"Ah, okay. Well, tell your daddy that Uncle Kent called."

"Okay. Love you," he says, and the call ends.

"Everything okay?"

"Yeah. Knox answered and said his mom is throwing up. My guess is morning sickness."

"I remember those days."

"Were you sick a lot while you were pregnant?"

"Not too bad, but there was a small stretch of about four weeks that it was pretty terrible. I'm not sure why they call it morning sickness when it's morning, noon, and night." She goes on to tell me about how she craved strawberry ice cream, and how hard it was to be having a baby by a man she couldn't remember.

"I'm going to be there for the next one."

"How do you think my husband will feel about that?" There is a sparkle in her eye that tells me she's kidding, but that's not a joking matter.

"I will feel damn proud to have created another tiny human with you."

She opens her mouth to reply but quickly closes it when there's a knock at the door. Leaning in, I kiss her quickly before going to the door. As soon as I pull the door open, Kendrix grins. "Daddy!" she cheers and leaps from my dad's arms to mine.

"Looks like Daddy's not the only one who carries you around," I say, stepping back to let them in.

"Papaw carries me," she answers.

"I can see that. Did you have fun?"

Her little head bobs up and down. "I played a whole bunch."

"Let's go see Mommy, and you can tell us all about it." I carry her into the living room and, with her on my lap, we sit next to Delaney on the couch and listen to her tell us how much fun she had at my parents.'

"Are you all ready to eat?" Mom asks.

"Let's go fill our bellies," I tell my daughter. She hops off my lap and rushes into the kitchen on my mom's heels.

"She's so happy," Delaney states the obvious.

I know this is hard for her. "She is." I stand and offer her my hand. "Let's go eat." I help her from the couch and to the kitchen table, ordering her to sit while I make her a plate. However, my mom is there, placing a plate in front of her.

"What would you like to drink? We have orange juice, water, milk, and I just put on a pot of coffee." Mom's eyes are kind as they settle on Delaney. Is that sadness I see? Worry? I can't describe the look she's giving her. I make a mental note to talk to her later.

184

"Orange juice, please, but I can get it," Delaney answers.

She tries to stand, but my mother holds up her hand to stop her. "No. You sit. You need your rest. Let me get it."

"Thank you, Georgia."

"You're welcome, sweetheart," Mom says, placing a glass of orange juice on the table in front of her.

Plates are emptied, and more drinks are poured as we sit around the table and talk. Kendrix carries most of the conversation. She's not leaving a single detail unturned as she tells us about her time at my parents' house.

Sitting back in my chair, I take it all in. My parents, my girls, all of us together. My family. I will forever mourn the time that I missed with them, but looking toward our future, this is what it's about. Moments in time when we're all together. She's staying. I don't have to worry about leaving the people I care about the most. I hate that my girls never had this—a strong support system, but they do now. I can't wait to see how our future unfolds.

⁂

"I need to call Mr. Garcia in the morning. With everything that happened yesterday, I didn't get to find out why he needed to talk to me," Delaney says as we're lying in bed Sunday night.

We finally got Kendrix to sleep in her room after three stories. I have no doubt she's going to end up in bed with us before the night is over. I need to get to work on setting her room up so she's more enticed to sleep there. She's never going to get any siblings if she keeps sleeping between us.

"He gave me something to give to you. I forgot about it until now. Hold on." Climbing out of bed, I make my way to the living room and grab the envelope from my coat pocket. I peek in on Kendrix, who is still sleeping soundly before heading back to our bedroom. "Here."

"What is it?"

"I don't know. He just told me to give it to you when you were up to it. He stopped by the hospital to check on you and handed it to me. I forgot about it until now."

185

She sits up in bed, resting her back against the headboard, and takes the envelope from my hands. I sit next to her on the edge of the bed, my hand on her thigh as I give her silent support. I can only assume that the letter is going to be from her father. Carefully, she opens the envelope and pulls out a folded sheet of paper and begins to read it out loud.

Delaney,

My darling daughter. I have too much to tell you, and yet as I sit here, I struggle to find the words. I have advised my attorney to not give you this letter until you'd had time to experience Jackson and the people who live here. Jackson holds a special place in my heart and always will. I don't know how I knew, but I had a feeling that I would need to insist on you visiting before selling, and I hope with all of my heart that you've found the missing piece of your past.

I don't really know how else to start other than to rip the Band-Aid off, so to speak. Here goes. If you're reading this, that means I've gone from this earth, resting with your grandparents and my love… your mother. There I said it. Tillie Nottingham is not your mother. I'm sorry that you are finding out like this, but I couldn't ever seem to find the courage to tell you in person. I didn't want to see the hurt or the disappointment in your eyes. Please don't hate me.

I'm sure you have many questions, and I'll do my best to clear them up for you now. Tillie and I were dating in college when she told me she was pregnant. I wasn't in love with her, but I wanted to do the right thing, Nottinghams always do the right thing. So I married her. Two months later, I was faced with the realization that she faked her pregnancy. The ink had long been signed on our marriage license, and I was at a loss. I was angry and hurt. In addition to that, I was young, but I wanted to be a father. I had grown fond of the idea and was crushed to find out the baby I had grown to love didn't exist.

I needed time away, so I came home to Jackson, Tennessee, to spend some time with my parents. It was there I met and fell in love with your mother—all in the span of two weeks' time. As I sit here writing this letter almost twenty-five years later, my heart still aches for her. She was and will forever be the love of my life.

I'm sure you're wondering what happened to her? I'll get to that, but first I need to tell you that I loved her. She was my heart and soul, and she loved you. She was so happy to be a mother. She talked about not being able to wait to hold you in her arms. You were her greatest accomplishment in life.

We had two incredible weeks together before I had to go back to my real life. Only what was once my real life was now fake. Nothing felt right, and my heart, it missed her. Two months went by, and your mother called to tell me about you. I immediately told Tillie that I wanted a divorce. I told her about your mother, Amber, and about you. She went crazy. She threatened to kill herself, and even tried to do so. I didn't know what to do. I was stuck, and your mother, she told me to get her through it. That we had a lifetime to be together. I wasn't sure it was the right choice, but that's what I did. I stayed. I took Tillie to see her therapist and went to counseling with her. All the while, admitting openly to her and her physicians that I didn't love her, that I would never forgive her, and that I wanted a divorce.

Fast forward a few months, and I get the call that your mother was in labor. I was going to be a father. I was three hours away and told her I would be there as soon as I could. Stubborn as she was, she thought she could drive herself to the hospital. Her best friend was out of town, and she had no one. My parents, your grandparents were

187

in Florida for the winter, and her parents, well, she never had a good relationship with them. So she said she's fine. She'd call me when she got there.

Two hours later, I was on the road, driving way past the speed limit to get to her. To get to you when my phone rang. Her best friend, Georgia, was on the other end crying hysterically. She was her emergency contact. There'd been an accident. She didn't have to tell me for me to know that it was bad. I could hear it in the tone of her voice, and I could feel it in my gut.

By the time I made it to the hospital, I was too late. Her injuries were too bad. She didn't make it, but they were able to save my daughter. You, Delaney. They were able to save you.

She's crying so hard that she hands me the letter. "Please, keep reading."

"Are you sure? Maybe we should take a break?"

"No, please, Kent. I need to hear it, but I can't see the pages." Her face is drenched with tears, and her eyes rimmed red and swollen.

I hate seeing her like this, but I'd do anything for her. Standing, I move from the edge of the bed, to fully sit next to her and pull her into my arms as I continue to read.

The love of my life was gone, and I was left with a piece of her, but I was lost. So damn lost. Tillie, she was there for me. She told me how sorry she was. She was sincere, and when I brought you home to the house that I shared with her, she helped me. She taught me to change a diaper and how to burp you. She went from ready to end her life to living. Living for you. You were a constant reminder that I stepped out on our marriage, yet she never held that against you. Not back then. She fell in love with you and presented me with a proposition. She raises you as her own. She cried for hours, telling me how sorry she was. How she always wanted to be a mother. I didn't forgive her, I couldn't, but if she hadn't done what she did, I never would have met your mother, and in turn, never would have had you. I know it sounds twisted but, in a way, she gave me you.

I didn't forgive her, but in time, I learned to live with the choices we had made. Neither of us was without our mistakes. I cheated on her. Regardless of what she did to me, that wasn't okay. We agreed to our new situation and lived our lives as best as we could.

I had a piece of your mother in you, and that was the greatest gift of all. You look so much like her, and as you got older, that resemblance increased. Life was good, we were happy, all of us, until my parents passed, and we moved to Jackson. Tillie had a hard time living in the house where I met your mother. She hated the town, hell, the entire state just for the simple fact it's where I was unfaithful.

As if the above story isn't bad enough, I still have more to say. Before I go any further, I want to tell you how sorry I am for keeping all of this from you. It was wrong, and I don't deserve your forgiveness. My only hope is that you find happiness and peace, and that your heart finds its love. When you find it, Delaney, when you find him, hold on tight and never let go.

I stop reading and place a kiss on her temple. "How you doing?"

"I can't believe this, Kent. All these years." Her voice cracks.

"You want me to stop? Maybe you've heard enough for today?"

"No. Keep going. I need to hear it. All of it."

"You sure?"

"Yes. Please." She peers up at me under long lashes that are wet from her tears. Her blue eyes are pleading and filled with the hurt that her father's words are causing her.

"I'm right here, baby. No matter what else we happen to uncover, I'm right here. It's you and me, you got that? You're not running away from me. I just got you back."

"I'm not going to run. I just… need to hear what else he's been hiding. I want it all out there so I can deal with it and move on."

"I love you." I kiss her temple one more time, before wrapping my arm a little tighter around her as I continue to read on.

> *The day of your accident, it all came rushing back to me. The day I lost your mother, the day you were born. I was in a dark place. I felt guilty because I had just talked to you, and you were upset. There was this guy, Kenton. You were in love with him, but he stood you up. I knew you were upset. I should have made you pull over until you were calmed down. I should have told you to stay put and that I would come and get you, but I did neither. Instead, I was talking to you. Listening to you talk about how great this guy was, and how you were sure he was on the same page, until he never showed up. Apparently, you saw his truck at the local bar in town, and you were frantic. You had to get back to school. You weren't willing to wait, so you left that night. You came home and packed your things and there was no stopping you. Tillie and I were at a fundraiser a few towns over. I should have left. I should have come to you, but I stayed and while I was talking to you, trying to calm you down, you were hit.*

> *I'll spare you the details of what I heard, but it hit me deep in my soul. I was going to lose you just like I lost her, and I couldn't deal. Tillie took over. She got us to the hospital; she handled it all. I was checked out… lost inside myself, inside my pain. By the time I knew what was happening, she had concocted this lie about how he didn't want you or your baby. We fought about it, but she swore she wasn't losing someone else she loved to that town or the trash in it. I didn't have any fight left in me, so I let her do what she wanted. I'd made so many mistakes in my life. I questioned everything, even my ability to protect you. Tillie convinced me this was the best way. That we*

would move to California to be closer to you, and we would help you raise your baby. She had no idea if or even when you would get your memories back and she said she would deal with it when it happened. I let her, and for that, I am deeply sorry.

I know that I kept you from your love, and my granddaughter from her father. I can't tell you what kind of man he is, because I never met him. I never gave him the chance to do the right thing. My hope is that you've found your way back to him and that the two of you are able to be together. That together, you can raise your daughter. Please tell him I'm sorry. I'm just at as much fault as Tillie, and keeping the truth from you is my greatest regret in life. I'm a coward, Delaney. I couldn't face you. I hope that the truth sets your heart free.

Please kiss my granddaughter for me. And if I may have one more request? Follow your heart, Delaney. Don't let my bad decisions affect your future. Live your life. Love like it's your last day, and live with no regrets. Trust me on this one, they haunt you.

I'll forever be watching over you, my darling daughter.

Love,

Dad

Dropping the letter to the bed, I wrap both arms around her as she sobs. I hold her until the tears have gone dry, and she's cried herself to sleep. Carefully sliding out of bed, I turn off the light, and then climb back in beside her, pulling her into my embrace. I can't imagine what she's feeling right now. I'm mad as hell for what they've done to us, but more so to her. She's lived her entire life thinking Tillie was her mother.

It takes me hours to fall asleep, too concerned she's going to wake up and need me, and I won't know. I don't know how to help her through this, but I can guarantee I will love her through it. We will rally around her and give her any and all support that she needs. I make a mental note to call in the troops as I finally drift off to sleep.

Chapter 21

Delaney

I've spent the last week going through the motions. I've read my father's letter at least a hundred times. Hell, by this point, I have it memorized. When I woke up from my accident and couldn't remember anything or anyone, it was scary. As the memories came back, that fear started to fade. This, however, knowing my entire life has been a lie? I hate that it was those years I don't remember. Why is my brain blocking the only real thing I've ever had? Why am I blocking Kent?

I've been having more and more flashbacks—or what I assume are memories of our time together. I'm grateful for a glimpse, but I want them all. He's my anchor in all of this, and when he looks at me, I can see the love in his eyes. When he tells me he loves me, I feel it deep in my soul. I want to say it back. I know it's been a very short time, but like Dad said in his letter, there is no real limit on when or how you fall in love. He fell in love with my mother, my real mother, Amber, in just two weeks.

Kent's friends and family have been incredible. I get calls daily asking for Kendrix to come over for playdates. Both Kendall and Mara have invited her over. Reagan stopped by with the boys, and the kids played while she listened to me yammer on about my life. Poor pitiful me. She assured me it was fine. Yesterday, Dawn showed up with Daisy and we went to lunch. They've rallied around me.

Today is Friday, and Kent's mom just called asking Kendrix and me to come over for lunch. I don't know if she is *the* Georgia in my father's letter, but I'm bringing it with me. I plan to ask her and see what she knows. What she can tell me. Maybe she can help fill in the gaps. Kent and I talked about it, and he wanted to call her that next day, but I wasn't ready. I needed some time to just process all the new information. I'm about five minutes from their place when my phone rings.

"That's your phone, Momma," Kendrix tells me from the back seat.

"I know, sweetie. We're almost to Mamaw and Papaw's, so I'm going to let it go to voice mail and call them back." What I don't tell her is that it's Tillie. The woman she believes to be my mother, her grandmother. I guess she still is. She's my stepmother, and I care for her, Kendrix loves her, but I'm angry and confused and I just can't deal with her right now.

Pulling into Georgia and Gordon's driveway, I grab my purse and Kendrix's backpack and help her out of her seat. Hand in hand, we walk to the front door and it opens before we can knock. Georgia is standing there with tears in her eyes. Her arms engulf me in a hug while I hear Gordon ask Kendrix if she wants to see something special. I feel his hand on my shoulder, and the weight of Kendrix's bag disappears, and then so do they.

"Come in." Georgia keeps her arm around me and guides me into the house. Kicking off my shoes and hanging up my coat, I follow her into the living room. "Kent called me last night. He said that you've been having a tough week. I badgered him until he told me." She smiles kindly, and it warms my heart. Georgia Baldwin is one of the most genuine people you will ever meet.

"You look just like her, like Amber. I saw her in you the first day Kent brought you home. I wanted to tell you, to drag out my pictures and tell you stories about her, but it wasn't my place. I wasn't sure if you knew, and I didn't want to open that can of worms and upset your life. I'm sorry. I feel as though maybe I made the wrong choice."

"No. You did the right thing. I needed to hear it from him. From my dad. There has been so much of my life that's been filled in by others, and even though this is his retelling, it's his truth. I needed that."

"She loved you, Delaney. Your mother, she loved you so much. I'd never seen her more excited for anything than becoming a mother. She was good to do it on her own too. She loved your father, but she had made peace with the fact that he was married. It wasn't something that they planned; it just happened. He told her he was separated and getting a divorce. In his heart, I know that's what he wanted."

I swallow hard. "You mentioned pictures. Do you still have them?"

She reaches over and grabs an old photo album from the coffee table. "She was my best friend. We did everything together. She was in my wedding." She hands me the album and scoots closer to me, where we're sitting on the couch. She begins to point out my mother and explain what was going on in each picture.

Tears slide down my cheeks and I quickly swipe them away. "I can't let her see me like this."

"Oh, don't you worry about that. Gordon and I set up her bedroom here, so he's going to have her occupied in there for a while."

"You set up a bedroom for her?"

"Of course we did. She's our granddaughter."

The way she says it. It's so simple to her, and I've never been more grateful to have people like her, like Gordon, and like Kenton in my life.

"You know we always said our kids could get married, and then we would have to be in each other's lives forever."

"Really?"

"Yeah. We had it all planned out." She laughs.

I don't know how long we sit here, looking through that album. Georgia tells me story after story about my birth mother, the times that they had. Gordon and Kendrix leave to go see Kent at work, and Georgia and I, we talk. All afternoon we talk and laugh. Not just about my mother, but about Kent when he was young. About motherhood, and just life.

Somewhere along the way, I realize I can't let myself dwell on the past. Sure, the details of my father's letter were unexpected, but the odds of me getting direct answers beyond that is slim to none. I need to leave the past where it is—the past. I need to look toward the future with Kenton and our daughter. With all these amazing people who have come into my life and have shown me what it's like to have a true support system, not one of manipulation. I'm tired of living in the unknown, the "let's wait and see." I want to live for me. Memories or not.

"I love him." I say the words out loud for the first time.

"I know you do."

"What?"

Georgia smiles. "Anyone can see it. You might not have your memories of your time with my son, but your heart, it remembers. I see it when you look at him." She places her hand on my arm and gives it a gentle squeeze. "Follow your heart, Delaney. Let it guide you. The best things in life are uncertain. They're scary, and it's a risk, but the rewards, they're worth it."

"Thank you for this." I hold up the now-closed photo album. "Thank you for today and talking to me about her, and just… listening. I needed this."

"You know where to find me if you need me. Besides, you're family now."

"You want to go over to the house? Meet up with Kendrix and Gordon?"

"Yes! It's been ages since I've seen the work the boys do."

I laugh. "Boys?"

"They will always be five years old in my eyes. Every single one of them. Come on, let's grab our coats."

"Wow," I say, walking into the kitchen. I haven't been here all week, too wrapped up in my own grief, if that's what you want to call it. It's amazing what five days can do for a demolished kitchen.

"Momma!" Kendrix calls out for me. She wiggles out of Kent's arms and comes rushing toward me. She crashes into my legs, hugging them tightly. "It's so pwetty."

Smoothing her hair back from her eyes, I agree with her. "It is."

"Laney." Kent's deep voice greets me. I look up, and he's before me, pressing his lips to mine.

"This is so much better than I imagined it."

"Thanks." Seth smirks.

"Hey, now." Mark laughs. "You're not exactly a one-man show."

"You can't help but follow in the footsteps of my awesome."

"Someone better call his wife," I tease. "Looks like she's going to need help getting his inflated ego through the door."

"Laney, you wound me." He places his hand over his heart as if his chest is hurting.

"I was actually getting ready to call you," Ridge says. "We're done here. We have to clean up, but the final step is flooring. We're starting on that Monday. We should be out of your hair next week."

"I can't believe it's done."

"You decide what you're going to do with it yet?" Tyler asks.

I look up at Kent, who is standing next to me with his arm around my shoulders. "Are we living here or somewhere else?" The words seem to shock him, and in a way, they do me as well. I guess my talk with Georgia did more than I thought. I want to be with him. I don't need an explanation or an excuse.

He recovers from my question and bends to press his lips to mine. "I'm wherever you and Kendrix are."

"Can you see yourself living here?"

"Yes," Ridge, Tyler, Mark, and Seth answer for him.

"Hell yes," Gordon adds.

"Papaw!" Kendrix scolds him.

"Sorry, princess. Papaw was just excited."

"Bad wowds."

"I know. I'll do better." He kneels down and opens his arms, and she doesn't hesitate to go to him.

"Out of all the men in this room, you were the last one I thought I had to worry about washing your mouth out with soap," Georgia teases.

"Ew." Kendrix scrunches up her nose, making us all laugh.

"Well, it looks like we're moving in," I say with excitement that I don't bother to hide.

"Excuse us," Kent says, then lifts me into his arms and carries me down the hall to the bedroom. Laughter follows us down the hall. When we're in the bedroom, he sets me on my feet. All the furniture in the room is pushed to the middle, which allowed them to add a fresh coat of paint. "What was that?"

"What?" I'm being coy and we both know it.

"That." He points toward the kitchen. "Us, moving in here. Tell me what that means, Laney."

"Well, usually when a man and a woman love each other, they do this kind of thing." I don't realize what I've said until the words leave my mouth. Not that I regret them. I just didn't expect to tell him like this.

"What did you just say?"

"That couples do this type of thing all the time."

"Laney." His voice is playful yet warning at the same time.

"Oh, you mean the when a man and a woman love each other? That part?"

"That's the one. I need you to tell me straight up."

"I love you, Kenton Baldwin. I might not have our memories, but my heart does." I repeat his mother's words from earlier. She said it beautifully.

"Take off your jeans," he says, walking backward toward the door. When he reaches it, he flicks the lock.

"What? We can't do that... here. Our daughter and your parents, and your friends are just down the hall."

"Our daughter will be kept occupied by your future in-laws and our friends. And you, my love, will just have to be quiet. Strip."

"So I tell you I love you, and you think you can boss me around?" There is no heat in my words.

"I think that you're my future wife and that I need to be inside you. Right. Now."

"So we skipped girlfriend. Because from what you've told me, we never had that title."

"Because you were always more than that. Strip."

"So this future wife business, let's talk about that."

"We will. But first." He unzips his jeans, pulling them and his underwear down, letting them pool at his knees. He takes his hard cock in his hand and strokes. "I need to be inside you, Laney. Now."

"What if I'm not quiet?"

"They'll distract her."

"What about them?"

He throws his head back and laughs. "They know we're sleeping together."

"You don't know that."

"I do know that." He closes his eyes as he strokes himself. "Laney, they know I love you. They know you're my forever. They know that even though the odds were stacked against us, we made our way back to each other. They also know I'm not an idiot. They know I crave to be a part of you."

"H-How do they know that?" His words are turning me on, and suddenly this little game to get him riled up has turned on me, and I'm ready for him. That's why I'm unbuttoning my jeans and sliding them and my panties off, kicking them aside.

"Because they know I love you."

"What are you waiting for?" His eyes pop open, and the dark brown orbs are full of desire. I take one step, then another, then another until I'm standing so close our bodies are touching.

"Arms around my neck, baby." He doesn't give me time to reply before he lifts me in the air. My arms and legs lock around him, and he pushes inside me. "Fuck." He buries his face in my neck as he slowly pushes in and out of my body. "It feels so... fuck. Condom."

"I'm on the pill."

"We'll talk about why later. You sure?"

"Don't you dare stop. My monthly cycle was all messed up after Kendrix. It helps to keep it regulated."

"Never been bareback."

"Never?"

He lifts his head to look at me. "No. The only one I ever would have considered it with was you, and we never did. We never discussed it."

"Well, now we are. Since I'm going to be your wife and all." I wink at him and he smirks. "Let's just agree to toss them. This, it feels way too good."

"Deal. Now, hold on tight and be quiet." I barely have time to lock my hands behind his neck before his relentless thrusts have me immobilized. "C-Close. Can't hold on," he grunts.

"I-I'm close. I can't be quiet. Oh, God." I moan from how good it feels, and that we're about to be discovered.

"Bite down on my shoulder."

"I can't bite you."

"It's either that or let them know I'm fucking you." Holding me with one hand, he slides the other between us and swipes it over my clit. He walks us toward the wall, and he presses me against it.

"The paint."

"It's dry. We did this room first." He unleashes… all I can do is hold on. Between his cock and his fingers, I have no option but to do as he says and bite down on his shoulder as my body convulses around him. "Fuck," he grunts, and I feel him as he releases inside me.

"That," I say, sucking in some much-needed air. "We should do more of that."

He throws his head back in laughter as he pulls his body from mine. "Let's get you cleaned up and we can do more of that when we get home tonight."

"When can we move in? I meant what I said. If you're okay with it, I'd like to live here. It's paid for, and with my inheritance, we wouldn't have to worry about the taxes eating our life savings away."

"We can move in as soon as the floors are finished. Do we need to go to California to get your stuff? Kendrix's stuff?"

"I'll call Mo—Tillie." I'm angry with her, and with my father. Calling her mom or mother right now, I just can't do it. I have too much in my head that I need to work out in regard to her. "I need to talk to her anyway. Hopefully, she'll have it shipped here. If not, I'll go get the important things like photos and mementos from when Kendrix was a baby. Everything else is just clothes and can be replaced."

"She's still in town. Her rental car is still at the hotel."

"Do you think your mom will watch Kendrix tonight? I can ask her to meet us here?"

"You know she will. Let's get cleaned up and we can ask her."

With a roll of paper towels, we do the best we can to clean up. The linens are all in totes so that the bathroom could be painted. We do okay with what we have. Back in the kitchen, the adults give us knowing looks, and my face heats, but I try to ignore it. He is the father of my daughter after all. That's how she got here.

"Mom, do you think you can watch Kendrix for a little while tonight?"

"Oh, I spend the night." Kendrix bounces on the balls of her feet. "Papaw, can we build another fort?'

"Sure, we can," Gordon quickly agrees.

"How about we ask Uncle Ridge and Uncle Seth if Finley and Everly can come too? You girls can all have a sleepover," Georgia suggests.

"Yeah!" Kendrix cheers.

"Sounds good to me," Ridge comments.

"Me too," Seth agrees.

"It's settled then. Sleepover at our house," Georgia tells our daughter.

The guys give Georgia and me a walk-through of the house, and I love it. There is nothing I would change. They did exactly as I wanted, only it's better than I imagined it could be. I can't seem to calm the giddy excitement that this is my home. Mine and Kent's. This is where we're going to raise our daughter and any future children. It feels right, all of it. The house, the man, the moment, it all feels right.

Chapter 22

KENT

"Come on in," I tell Tillie as I answer the door. She doesn't sneer at me or try to scratch my eyes out, so I call that progress. "Laney's in the kitchen." She walks away from me and heads that way. I follow along behind her. Laney asked me to be here for this, and nothing Tillie says is going to keep me from doing just that.

"Tillie," Delaney greets her.

"Is that any way to greet your mother?"

"Stepmother," Delaney corrects, and lets that hang in the air between them.

"What did you do?" She turns and glares at me.

"It was Dad. He left me this." She holds up the letter. "I get it now. The reason you wanted to control me. I understand that you hated this town and this house. But Kent, he did nothing to you. You kept my daughter from her father for your own selfish reasons. You robbed the three of us of so many years."

203

"Oh, and I suppose your father is innocent in all of this? And him"—she points at me—"his mother and her," she spits, "were close. I knew they would tell you."

"See, that's where you're wrong, Tillie. Georgia recognized me right away, but she never said a word. She never let on, not once. Not until I read the letter from Dad, and she found out he had told me the truth. I understand he cheated on you. I can respect the fact that you were hurt and angry. I'm grateful you stepped in as my mother under those circumstances."

I watch Tillie closely and see the cracks in her armor. Her shoulders deflate just a little and the scowl on her face is less prominent.

"Thank you for raising me. Sure, you were a little controlling."

I hide my grin, pretending to cover a cough at my girl's dig.

"But you were good to me. That is until you weren't. I can't remember the days when Kent and I were dating. Not really. I'm having more and more flashbacks, but the truth still remains the same. You lied to me. You kept me from him, and him from us. You sabotaged my family."

"I was your family!" Tillie yells. "Me. I raised you. I loved you. He was going to take you away from me."

"No, Tillie. He wasn't. That never would have happened. You were selfish. You didn't want to have the memories thrown in your face, so you lied. You manipulated me. You took advantage of the fact that I lost my memory. You made me think he was a bad man when he's anything but. His friends, his family, they're all incredible people who enrich our lives. Kendrix and I have had their love and support from day one."

"He's feeding you lies."

"No. My father... that's who you're upset with. I understand that too, but you chose to stay. You chose to raise me as your own. You chose to lie to me. Those choices, they were all yours. You ruined our relationship. Not Kent and not my father. That was all on you."

"So, what? That's it? I'm no longer your mother? I'm not welcome in your life? What about K—my granddaughter?"

"See." Delaney points at her. "You still can't even say her name. A name that is so much like her father's. Even not knowing him, I named our baby after him. That's love, Tillie. Deep-rooted, forever-in-your-soul love."

My need to touch her outweighs anything else. I move in closer, where we're both standing with our backs leaning against the kitchen counter, and slide my arm around her waist. "I love you," I whisper, my lips next to her ear.

"I love you too." Her voice is loud and clear. No hesitation.

"You're all I have," Tillie says, her voice cracking.

Finally, her stone-cold façade is slipping. Delaney leans into me, and I stand strong, offering her support.

"You should have thought about that sooner. I'm staying here, Tillie. I'm keeping the house. Kent and I are going to live here, with our daughter."

"What does that mean?"

"That means that I'm not coming home to California. I would appreciate it if you would ship our things, but if not, I'll make the trip and do it myself."

"I'll never see you."

"You know where I live."

"I hate this town."

Delaney shrugs. "I don't know what to tell you. I can't just forgive and forget what you did to us. I'm not saying never, but I am saying not right now. If you want to see your granddaughter, because through it all, to her you're her grandmother, you're going to have to come here. I don't feel comfortable leaving you alone with her."

"I never meant to hurt you, Delaney. I was scared of losing you, and I needed you to listen."

"So you yank on my hair, causing me to slip on the ice and be knocked unconscious? You know I can press charges against you, right? That what you did was assault?"

Her eyes well with tears. "Yes, and I'm so terribly sorry. I never meant to hurt you."

"What exactly are you sorry for?" Delaney asks, her hands resting on her hips.

"All of it," she whispers.

"We have plenty of space. You're welcome to stay with us," I speak up. Even through everything, she's still the only mother and until recently grandmother my girls had in their life. I'm a glass-half-full kind of guy, and I hope one day we can all be on better terms.

"He's right. You are welcome here, with some conditions."

"Which are?"

"You speak not a word of this to Kendrix. You accept Kent as my future husband, and you accept Kendrix as his daughter. That goes for her name as well."

"Delaney." Tillie's voice is pleading.

"No. We've played by your terms for far too long. I'm taking back my life. Starting now. Take it or leave it."

The room is silent for several minutes when Tillie finally nods. "I'll ship your things."

"Thank you. I'll send movers to come and pack it all up. I just need you to let them in."

"Can I see her? Before I leave, can I see my granddaughter?" She swallows hard. "C-Can I see K-Ken-Kendrix?"

"I think she'd like that."

Tillie nods. "Thank you."

"Will you two be okay here? I'll run to my parents' and pick up our girl."

"Thanks, babe. We'll be fine. Drive safe."

"Love you." I kiss her quickly and rush out the door.

By the time I'm back, Delaney and Tillie have managed to whip up some spaghetti for dinner, and have plates set out at the island.

"Grandma!" Kendrix rushes toward Tillie and hugs her legs tightly. "You's been gone fowever."

"I know, sweetie. Grandma has been giving you time with your daddy." Her eyes flash to mine then back to my daughter.

"Oh, I love my daddy. I gots a mamaw and papaw too."

"I heard that. I'm so happy for you, Kendrix."

Delaney sucks in a breath, and when I look at her, I see tears in her eyes. It's then that I know everything is going to be okay. The odds may have been stacked against us, and the future uncertain, but we battled our way through.

Unexpected Odds

Life has thrown us some curveballs, and there have been times when the unexpected changes have literally knocked us on our ass. We've had to learn to live one breath, one second, one minute, one hour, one day at a time. We learned that the best things in life are truly unexpected. We've embraced it and learned to live with our unexpected odds.

Epilogue

Delaney

Today is a special day for so many reasons. Let's start with the fact that my little girl turns five. I can't believe how fast time has passed. She's been talking about today, her princess party, for the last two weeks. She's not the only one who's excited. Her daddy, my fiancé, he's also a bouncing ball of energy. This is the first birthday he's gotten, and he ran with it. Our house looks like someone puked pink and purple, and I'm pretty sure we'll be sweeping up glitter for months. I've let him plan and make this day so extravagant I don't know how we'll ever top it. So yeah, that makes today extra special.

"I gotta admit," Reagan says with her hand on her growing belly bump. "I never thought I'd see Kent all pinked out." She chuckles.

I'm sitting with the wives, Kendall, Reagan, Dawn, and Mara, while the guys finish with the decorations. "He's a big softie."

"Oh, they all are," Mara agrees.

"Honestly, I still find it hard to believe there are five of them. Five guys, the best of friends, and all great catches. They love us and our children fiercely, yet still manage to look like badasses."

"Shh." Dawn laughs. "Don't let them hear you. They don't need their egos stroked."

"I don't know." Kendall rubs her baby bump. "We should give credit where credit is due." She points down at her belly, and we all break out into a fit of giggles.

The guys look over at us, each one of them only having eyes for the leading lady in their lives. Kent's eyes sparkle with happiness as he winks at me.

"Let me see that rock again." Reagan reaches for my hand and places it on her pregnant belly. "He did good. He did damn good," she praises.

"You guys really didn't know?" I ask them.

"Not a word. Ridge came home with Kendrix saying we were watching her so you all could get the house ready for the party and that Kent wanted it to be a surprise," Kendall explains. "I called him out on it when we got here, and you all told us you were engaged. He knew!"

"Oh, they all knew," Reagan tells us. "Tyler sang like a canary. Apparently, it's the pregnancy hormones or something. He said he was scared for his life." She cackles.

"We're lucky," Dawn says wistfully. "Sure, I mean, so are they, but really, we're lucky. It's rare to find a love like we all have, and look at us. All five of us have found it. Not only that, but it brought the five of us together. I cherish that, and each of you."

"Damn pregnancy hormones." Mara laughs, wiping her eyes.

"What?" Kendall shrieks. "Are you?"

Mara's face goes beet red. "I meant Dawn."

"Nope. Spill it, sister."

"Fine, yes, we're pregnant. I'm freaking out. Ryder will be thirteen months old when the baby gets here. That's two under age two, plus an almost four-year-old. What were we thinking?"

"You weren't. It's that sweet yet alpha voodoo they put on us. Don't act like you don't know what I'm talking about." Reagan points at each of us.

"I love that all four of us are pregnant at the same time. If I didn't know any better, I'd think the guys planned it," Kendall jokes.

"What about you?" Reagan looks over at me. "Any thoughts about adding to the Baldwin brood?"

I open my mouth to speak and then close it. I do this twice more before these ladies, my friends, figure me out.

"No!" Dawn says excitedly.

"Shh. I haven't told him yet."

"Why not?" Mara asks, concern in her voice.

"I found out for sure yesterday. Then last night when I got home, Kendrix was gone, and he had flowers and candles and all the sweet romantic 'I want you to have my last name' stuff, and he was so proud of himself for pulling it off without me finding out. I had no clue, none whatsoever. I didn't want to take away from his night."

"I know you missed your chance with that the first time around," Kendall says gently. "But, he's just like the others. That news wouldn't have taken away from the night, but it would have added to it."

"I know. I just chickened out, I guess. I know he loves me and he's been open and honest about having more kids. I don't know. I just froze up and didn't tell him."

"Well, what do you say we keep an eye on Kendrix, and you tell him now?"

"I'm going to tell him tonight." What I don't tell them is that I have something else to tell him. I had a dream the night before last. We were in the meadow, lying on a blanket. His arms were wrapped around me as he whispered, "I missed you," into my ear. It was summer break from college, and my first day back in Jackson. We made love in the open field, and he held me the entire day. It was perfect. When I woke up, it wasn't just a dream. It was my life. *Our* life. It all came rushing back to me like a flood. Even the night he didn't show up. I was scared to tell him I was pregnant. We had never identified what we were to each other. I didn't know how he was going to take it and then he never showed up.

Crushed, I left town early. I still had every intention of telling him about the baby. I never would have kept it from him. It was his choice to make if he wanted to be in our lives. His and his alone.

I admit that a little of my apprehension in telling him comes from that night, but he's proven over and over again that's not who he is. He loves Kendrix with everything he is, and me too. I know my worry is silly, but it's there all the same.

"Nope. You need to do it now. The parents won't be here for—" Dawn looks at her watch. "—another thirty minutes. We've got the kids, everything is done, the guys are just messing with streamers to look busy." We all laugh at that because it's the truth. "Go tell him now. We've got this."

"I don't want to take away from Kendrix and her first birthday with her daddy."

"Laney," Mara chimes in. "You're going to tell her that she's going to be a big sister and that her daddy is for certain going to be here for all the birthdays to come. That's not taking away from her big day."

"Go." Reagan's voice is stern.

"Damn, Tyler was right. Those pregnancy hormones are scary," I tease her.

"Oh, hush." She snorts. "Go."

"All right. I'm going. Let him tell the guys."

"You got it. That's what they get for not letting us in on the engagement." Kendall grins.

"Wish me luck," I say as I stand from the couch.

"You don't need it," the four of them call back.

Here goes nothing.

Epilogue

KENT

It doesn't matter where she is in the room, my eyes seek her out. The connection we have is that strong. That's why I tune out of the conversation Ridge is having about something cute as hell that Knox said about Kendall being pregnant when she stands and heads this way.

She's glowing, and I know it's from happiness, and from the baby she's carrying. I'm more in tune with her body than my own. She missed her last cycle, and her breasts have been tender. Trust me, I know because I give them lots and lots of attention. She also asked my mom to watch Kendrix yesterday. She had an appointment. One I was unaware of. I don't need her to tell me to know that she's pregnant. I thought maybe last night would be the night she would tell me.

At first, I was worried she would think my knowing about her pregnancy was why I proposed, but that sounds ridiculous even to my own ears. I've told her since the day she declared she wanted us to live here that she was going to be my wife. I've also made it known that I'm more than ready to add to our family.

"Hey, baby." I snake an arm around her waist and pull her into me.

"Hi. Can you help me with something?"

"Laney!" Seth scolds. "There are children present." He can barely say it with a straight face.

"I know. All of your wives are going to keep an eye on them for me. Don't worry. I'll bring him right back."

"Kent, brother. There's medication for that," Tyler teases.

I discreetly flip him my middle finger and follow Laney down the hall to our bedroom. "What's up?" I ask her.

"Well, there's something I need to tell you. I was going to wait, but there's no time like the present, right?"

"Right," I agree.

She steps into me, rests her head on my chest, and wraps her arms around my waist. "I love you, Kenton."

"I love you too." I run my hands up and down her back, soothing her.

"I didn't expect this. This life we're building. I remember," she says softly.

"You remember what, baby?"

She pulls back, and big blue eyes peer up at me. "I remember us," she says as a tear slides down her cheek.

This, I was not expecting. "Okay. What does that mean? I promise you, I'll never stand you up. Never. Laney, I'm so sorry," I start to apologize again. I've done it several times over since we've been back together.

"Stop. You're a good man, Kent. I know that even without my memories. Having all of that, it just makes this moment even more special. I remember every touch, every caress. Everything. I remember it all."

"When?"

"Yesterday."

"Why didn't you tell me?"

She shrugs. "I was too busy going through it all in my mind, and then when I got home, the house was so beautiful, and I didn't want to make the day about me and my past. I wanted it to be about us and our future."

"Us. Laney. It's always us. You can tell me anything. Anytime."

"I almost didn't tell you today. It's such a special day. Our little girl is turning five, you're here for the first birthday with her, and many more to come." She adds, "I have my memories back."

"How? When? Tell me everything."

"Well, before I can tell you that, I have something else to tell you."

This is it. Here it comes. The moment I missed out on with Kendrix.

"I'm pregnant."

I lift her into my arms and kiss her. "I fucking love you so damn much."

"You're happy?" she asks when I finally set her on her feet.

"Ecstatic."

"Well, I was at the OB yesterday to confirm my suspicion, and the moment the doctor walked into the room, it was like déjà vu. It all came rushing back to me. The same doctor, the same situation. When he told me I was pregnant, the same scene almost six years ago flashed through my mind.

"That night, I did have something to tell you. Two things. I wanted to tell you that I was in love with you. I knew you loved me too; I could feel it. Then I was going to tell you that you were going to be a daddy. I was going to transfer for my last year of college and move here. I wanted to start building our life together."

"I'm so sorry I wasn't there when I said I would be."

"It's all in the past. What we have to look forward to is our future, as a family of four."

"Oh, we're not stopping at two."

"No?"

"Nope. This is a big-ass house, Laney. We have to fill it up."

She laughs. "Well, Tillie has a room for when she stays here."

Tillie has been making an effort to be the person she should have been all those years ago. Delaney still has her guard up. It's going to take some time, but I think she'll get there.

"Okay. We have six bedrooms. We have at least two more babies to add to the clan."

"Let's get this one here and we can talk about more."

"Deal." I kiss her softly. "So, when are you going to be my wife?"

"How's tomorrow sound?"

"What?"

"Justice of the peace. I just want to be married. We've lost so much time. I don't need the flair of a wedding or the fancy dress. I just need your last name. Besides, if Kendrix is a Baldwin, I want to be too."

"What do you mean?"

"Oh, did I forget to tell you? I told you today was special for all kinds of reasons." She flashes me a smile, and I feel as though my heart is about to beat out of my chest. "I got the final paperwork. I added you as Kendrix's father on her birth certificate and officially changed her last name. Just in time for kindergarten in the fall."

"She's Kendrix Baldwin."

"She is."

I crush her to my chest in a hug. I just want to hold her. The chance of me finding the one that got away was uncertain. In fact, the odds weren't exactly in my favor. However, here we are. It's unexpected but no less than perfect. I'll place my bet on the unexpected odds every time.

Thank you for taking the time to read

Unexpected Odds

Never miss a new release:
http://bit.ly/2UW5Xzm

More about Kaylee's books:
http://bit.ly/2CV3hLx

Contact
KAYLEE RYAN

Facebook:
http://bit.ly/2C5DgdF

Instagram:
http://bit.ly/2reBkrV

Reader Group:
http://bit.ly/2o0yWDx

Goodreads:
http://bit.ly/2HodJvx

BookBub:
http://bit.ly/2KulVvH

Website:
www.kayleeryan.com

Other Works
BY KAYLEE RYAN

With You Series:

Anywhere With You | More With You | Everything With You

Soul Serenade Series:

Emphatic | Assured | Definite | Insistent

Southern Heart Series:

Southern Pleasure | Southern Desire | Southern Attraction | Southern Devotion

Unexpected Arrivals Series:

Unexpected Reality | Unexpected Fight
Unexpected Fall | Unexpected Bond | Unexpected Odds

Standalone Titles:

Tempting Tatum | Unwrapping Tatum | Levitate
Just Say When | I Just Want You
Reminding Avery | Hey, Whiskey | When Sparks Collide
Pull You Through | Beyond the Bases
Remedy | The Difference
Trust the Push

Co-written with Lacey Black:

It's Not Over

Acknowledgements

To my readers:

Thank you for following me on this journey with the Beckett Construction Crew and their Unexpected Arrivals. I can't thank you enough for reading. I'm so glad that you loved these characters as much as I do. I'm sad to see them go, but I'm excited for all new worlds coming later this year.

To my family:

I love you. Thank you for believing in me, and being my number one supporter. I could not do this without you.

Wander Aguiar:

Thank you for an amazing image that brought Kent to life!

Jonny James:

I've been holding onto this image for a long time now. Just waiting for Kent's story to release. Thank you for doing what you do, so authors can bring their characters to life for readers.

Tami Integrity Formatting:

Thank you for making The Unexpected Odds paperback beautiful. You're amazing and I cannot thank you enough for all that you do.

Sommer Stein:

Time and time again, you wow me with your talent. Thank you for another amazing cover.

My beta team:

Jamie, Stacy, Lauren, Erica, and Franci I would be lost without you. You read my words as much as I do, and I can't tell you what your input and all the time you give means to me. Countless messages and bouncing idea, you ladies keep me sane with the characters are being anything but. Thank you from the bottom of my heart for taking this wild ride with me.

Give Me Books:

With every release, your team works diligently to get my book in the hands of bloggers. I cannot tell you how thankful I am for your services.

Tempting Illustrations:

Thank you for everything. I would be lost without you.

Julie Deaton:

Thank you for giving this book a set of fresh final eyes.

Becky Johnson:

I could not do this without you. Thank you for pushing me, and making me work for it.

Marisa Corvisiero:

Thank you for all that you do. I know I'm not the easiest client. I'm blessed to have you on this journey with me.

Kimberly Ann:

Thank you for organizing and tracking the ARC team. I couldn't do it without you.

Bloggers:

Thank you, doesn't seem like enough. You don't get paid to do what you do. It's from the kindness of your heart and your love of reading that fuels you. Without you, without your pages, your voice, your reviews, spreading the word it would be so much harder if not impossible to get my words in reader's hands. I can't tell you how much your never-ending support means to me. Thank you for being you, thank you for all that you do.

To my Kick Ass Crew:

The name of the group speaks for itself. You ladies truly do KICK ASS! I'm honored to have you on this journey with me. Thank you for reading, sharing, commenting, suggesting, the teasers, the messages all of it. Thank you from the bottom of my heart for all that you do. Your support is everything!

With Love,

Kaylee Ryan
AUTHOR